MY BIG SCALY ALIEN NAGA

STARLIGHT MONSTERS
BOOK 3

SKYE MACKINNON

Peryton Press

MY BIG SCALY ALIEN NAGA

SKYE MACKINNON

CONTENTS

Click – minute (30 Earth minutes are 20 intergalactic clicks)

Cycle – day (one IG day has 27 Earth hours; there are 10 IG days in an IG week)

Intergalactic Authority (IA) – law-enforcing organisation (space police), overseen by the Intergalactic Council

Kalumbu Station – the orbiting space station where the Trials are monitored and run.

Peritan – intergalactic term for a human

Peritus – intergalactic term for planet Earth

R'hat – a derogatory term for maintenance workers on Kalumbu Station

Rotation – one year in Intergalactic Standard

Serpenthyra – planet of the naga

VENOM

TWO ROTATIONS AGO

I hissed at the Kardarian who'd stepped on my tail. He flashed his fangs at me but then bowed his head and hurried off before I could take this confrontation further. Unlike Kardarians, I was at the top of the food chain.

I curled the tip of my tail under my coils where it couldn't be stepped on by distracted idiots. Sometimes, I purposely tripped my co-workers to start a fight, but I had a deadline and couldn't afford a brawl. Maybe tomorrow. I hadn't established my dominance in a while. It was always good to remind everyone why nagas were feared across the galaxy.

Turning back to my screens, I grimaced. Whoever had written this code was an even bigger idiot than most of my colleagues. It was easy to attract brainless grunts to work on an illegal space station, but finding qualified, educated individuals was almost impossible. It's why I'd been able to rise through the ranks so quickly.

If the head of my department hadn't been a niece of Jarra, the Prime Game Maker, I may have been in charge of the entire division by now. But as things stood, I'd reached the end of the ladder, at least for as long as Briarra was alive.

I may keep her that way. For now, she was useful to me. She hadn't got this job because of her skills, but because of her connections, giving me free reign to do whatever I wanted as long as I pretended that it had been her idea in the first place.

Code flowed across the screen, turning into colourful images before my inner eye. Where others only saw letters and numbers, I saw a story. I saw roads that could be followed and doors that could be opened. In all my studies, I'd never met anyone who reported to perceive code the way I did. To them, it was a job. To me, this was the voice of a friend speaking to me, telling me stories of all that was happening on the station.

I focused on the shields surrounding the planet. They kept any nosey visitors from flying down to Kalumbu's surface while at the same time shielding us from the authorities' eyes. Jarra spent a lot to bribe the Intergalactic Authority, but it was always better to be safe than sorry. The game makers didn't save on security expenses, which is why I had no qualms charging the hourly rates that I did.

The code was inefficient but surprisingly robust. I

swept through it, updating and patching. I should pitch a full redesign to Briarra soon – give myself the chance to hide even better loopholes than the ones I'd already built.

An alert caught my eye. A new shipment had arrived and was automatically being transported to the cargo bay. Wait, no. Not to cargo. There was a diversion in the code to have it moved somewhere else. A part of the station that I was sadly very familiar with.

I glanced around to make sure no one was watching, then opened a discreet window in the lower corner of my screen.

Live cargo. Fuck.

Another batch of victims for the Trials. Probably poached from unexplored planets or hijacked mid-transit by pirates. I activated a subroutine to log everything and store it on my secure, biolocked drive. No one but me could access it – not even if I was caught.

Not that I worried about discovery. Everyone here saw the naga, the fangs, the coils – and assumed I was just another predator. A criminal like all of them. No one questioned my loyalty. No one suspected I wasn't what I seemed.

I scrolled deeper into the cargo's data. Thirty cryopods. They'd been on a long journey, travelling for many intergalactic years. They'd changed hands so often that I couldn't see what planet they'd originally come from. Somehow, they'd made it to the Kalumbu space station, sold to the game makers by a trader specialising in live cargo. The captives were designated as female Peritans. I'd never come across that species before. Later, back in my tiny cabin, I'd read up on them, but right now, I didn't have the time for research.

I hijacked a surveillance drone, sending it to follow the shipment. Through the glass top of one pod, I glimpsed a face. Female.

My body went rigid. My fangs ached.

Mine.

Not property. Not prey.

Mate.

My one and only.

I knew it in my bones.

I forced myself to stay still. To keep breathing. If I hadn't been trained by the IA, I might've blown my cover right then. But I couldn't afford a mistake, even though every scale on my body seemed to itch with the urge to wrap myself around my mate.

She'd been in cryosleep for years. She could wait a few more hours.

I began to code. Line after line. A program to monitor her pod and every mention of her and the other females. Subtle. Hidden. Safe.

I'd see her soon.

I slithered into the storage chamber an hour after my shift, sensors cloaked, scent masked. The air in the room was sharp with frost, humming with the low vibration of cryopods stacked in towering rows.

I gave them only cursory glances. I couldn't help them all. One pod was open and empty. Had the Peritan died? I made a mental note to follow up on this later.

Only one female was important right now. Mine.

Her pod was positioned at the back, buried behind two others that had been shoved in haphazardly. Typical. These game makers didn't see value in their victims. Just product. Entertainment.

Very few workers ever came down here. A shiver ran over my scales. I wouldn't be able to stay for very long before my muscles turned sluggish and my brain fogged up. I hated the cold. Hated the thought that my mate was kept in such an inhospitable place.

My hearts beat faster the closer I got. I didn't really know what I'd do when I got there. I'd come up with a hundred different plans and then discarded them again. Freeing her from the pod was easy. The problem was what to do after. There was no way of getting her off the station, at least not right now. I could smuggle her into the next transport ship by changing their inventory system, but I couldn't come with her. Not until I'd completed my task here. As much as I craved being with my mate, my duty couldn't be ignored.

Despite the urgency, I approached slowly. This was a special moment. Of all the ways I'd imagined meeting my mate, this wasn't it. She had no idea I was even here. It felt wrong that I was able to see her, yet she was frozen in time, so deeply unconscious that she wasn't even dreaming. At least that's what I had been told about cryosleep. There were no pods suited for nagas, so I had never experienced it myself.

I brushed a speck of dust from the glass window above my mate.

She was so tiny.

The pod was made for aliens of all shapes and sizes, and she looked like barely a child in that metal monstrosity. They hadn't even put a sheet beneath her. Her frail body was lying on nothing but cold titanium.

I focused on her face first. So unlike my own. Her skin had no scales, fur or even hair, except for a few strands of curls the colour of the night sky that were almost entirely hidden under the straps that held her head in place.

Her two eyes were closed, hidden beneath silky lids. A cute little nose stood above voluptuous lips that I craved to touch. Her colouring reminded me of the mala trees on my home world. In the fire season, they bloomed a fierce red that stood in sharp contrast to the soothing browns of their trunks and leaves. The flowers exuded a slightly euphoric scent, which is why you'd often find young nagas curled around these trees, enjoying a natural high.

I leaned closer.

"Hello, mate," I whispered.

Her lips didn't move, but I thought I saw her

eyelids twitch. Still under. She wouldn't wake for a while yet. The pod was keeping her in stasis.

I ran a scan. No major injuries. Cryo-burn at minimal levels. Metabolism intact. Whoever handled her prep had done it right. Rare.

Gently, I rested my hand on the glass above her chest.

"I'll get you out," I said. "Not just from this pod. From everything. I promise."

Her body didn't stir. But I imagined she heard me anyway.

A strong shiver ran all along my body, reminding me that it was time to go. I'd be back as soon as I could. And I would come up with a plan to save my mate. We'd be together, somewhere far away from Kalumbu, somewhere safe.

I ran a fingertip along the curve of the pod, then forced myself to leave.

I had work to do.

ONE ROTATION AGO

I watched her every day. She always looked the same, preserved in a single moment by the cryopod. Her hair didn't grow, her scale-less skin never changed. She seemed peaceful, the ghost of a smile playing around her pale lips. Sometimes I saw the tiniest twitch at the edges of her eyes. Was she dreaming? I'd been told it was impossible, but she was a rare species. It might be different for her.

Peritans. That's what her kind was called.

I had not found much intel on them. A barely developed species on a backwater planet in a little explored part of the galaxy. Every time I looked at her, I wondered how she got here. Peritans had space travel, but they'd barely made it out of their own solar system. Not far enough to encounter space pirates. Maybe she'd been abducted from her planet. It happened. Slavers, crazy scientists, organ traders, other criminals who didn't care about intergalactic law.

On Kalumbu Station, I was surrounded by them. My mate, innocent and beautiful in her eternal sleep, was who kept me going.

I kept my tail extended further around my workstation than I usually would. If anyone got too close, I'd feel it. But even with that precaution, I forced myself to only look at her every few clicks. I had work to do, trying to finish the job as fast as possible. No matter that my bosses refused to listen to me when I told them that I wanted out. I wasn't known for listening to authority.

But not much longer and I would have gathered enough evidence. I'd complete the assignment as agreed, free my mate, and then it was up to them if they wanted to sack me or not. I had siphoned off enough credits to hidden accounts for my mate and I to live in relative prosperity on some faraway moon where property was still cheap. But first, I had to free her. I still hadn't figured out the best way to do so.

My latest idea was to blackmail my employer into helping both of us escape. Right now, the exit strategy only included me, but if I withheld crucial data from them, they might budge into creating a way for both of us to leave. But for that to happen, I had to continue to work in the shadows, keeping my head down and staying focused. If I got distracted, it would take longer for us to escape. Yet I couldn't help but visit her as often as I dared. And always, always, she was on my mind, burned into my soul.

───────

ONE MONTH AGO

I stared at the instructions, my hearts beating furiously. The next season of the Trials would include Peritan women as damsels in distress.

They'd been sleeping peacefully for almost two rotations. Three had died during that time because their cryopods failed. I thought the game makers had forgotten about them, but no, they'd simply been biding their time.

Five females had been chosen as the first victims. I compared their identification numbers in the system to the files I'd created on every single female. I'd started with a file on my mate, then continued recording the others' details. I would pass the information on to the authorities. Maybe that could be used to return them to their homes. Although I wasn't sure they'd want to go home when they found out how long they'd been in cryo. I dreaded having that conversation with my mate already.

They'd chosen some of the weakest females. Not even one who was a warrior or athlete or survival expert. The game makers clearly didn't want anyone who might stand a chance. And one of the five was my mate.

I was so tempted to change the game makers' instructions. Every cell in my body screamed at me to protect my mate. I couldn't let her be sent to the planet's surface. It was a death sentence. Yet I couldn't risk it. The game makers had chosen these females. They might remember who they chose and why. Any changes would be noticed.

I would have to let it come to pass. But that didn't mean I couldn't help. I had done that for other Trial participants, the ones that might stand a chance to win.

Hacking deeper into the data didn't take long. The first couple was a female called Fay and an orc named Vruhag. She was a lucky Peritan to have been paired with such a strong warrior species. I switched to the camera view of his cell. He was struggling against his restraints, his muscles bulging beneath thick green skin. He would be a formidable contestant. And with a bit of help, he might keep her alive for long enough.

A few more commands and I'd set myself up as an anonymous sponsor. I paid a ridiculous amount of credits to allow the orc the choice of a weapon. Orcs had natural weaponry, but a good sword or axe would increase his chances. There was nothing I could offer the female. Except...

An idea sprang to my mind. Yes, that could work.

It was time to contact the chii.

UNKNOWN

PRESENT TIME

He sweeps me into his arms and I squeal with laughter, leaning into his touch. I feel light in his presence, so very happy and contented, as if the world stops spinning every time we're together. All my worries fade away and I simply live in the present, just him and me, together. He whispers to me, words of love and adoration, and I soak them up and store them deep inside my heart. His strong arms are tight around me, a promise, protecting me from all that might trouble this moment. I kiss the side of his neck, a place where I know he is particularly sensitive, and he laughs, a grumbling sound that intertwines with my own joyful laughter perfectly. Time stops. This is for us. Just us. Our time. Our life. We belong together. I am his. He is mine.

Thought sparked into existence, a tiny flame barely illuminating the all-encompassing darkness. I knew that I was asleep, just about, but that's all I knew. My mind was sluggish, bumping against corners that shouldn't exist.

Who am I?

The question floated up, hazy and insistent. I reached for it, but it slipped through my fingers like smoke.

I fought to wake. Not fully, not yet, but enough to peel back the fog. My body felt distant – heavy and unreachable. My thoughts were dull and slow, dragging through molasses. This wasn't natural. This wasn't right.

It should've been easy. Wake up, start the day. But there was no day. No light. Just darkness and the soft echo of a self I couldn't remember.

I should have a name. A life. Memories. Something. But whenever I reached for them, I found only emptiness.

The flame of lucid thought was flickering more strongly as more questions rose to the surface. *Why can't I remember? Where has everything gone?*

Still, I pressed on. I became aware of my body, little by little. Limbs like lead, a mouth too dry to swallow, eyelids glued shut. But I was here. I existed. I felt.

Time lost meaning. Seconds stretched like years. Or maybe it was years.

The darkness didn't become any brighter, but my

awareness expanded a little further every time I was conscious enough to notice.

I was lying on something cold and hard. Even though I couldn't remember what my own bed felt like – assuming that I owned a bed – I was quite sure that this wasn't a mattress. A table, maybe. Using that realisation as an anchor, I tried to remember how I may have come to lie on a table. Nothing. My memories remained blank.

But the table was real and I held onto that. I was real.

Then pain.

Sharp and sudden, a jab in my wrist. I would have cried out if I'd had the strength. Heat bloomed through me like wildfire, licking up my arm and down my spine, flooding every nerve. Sweat erupted on my skin.

I gasped, or tried to. My chest heaved and my heart kicked harder, fighting the burn.

And something shifted. The fog cracked. The numbness thinned.

I wanted to live.

That simple truth blazed inside me, brighter than any memory.

I wanted to wake.

I wasn't ready yet. But I was closer.

Closer to answers.

Closer to freedom.

Closer to whoever had whispered to me in the dark.

. . .

My eyes snapped open.

Light poured in – sharp, sterile, white. I flinched and immediately regretted it. Pain stabbed behind my eyes and my stomach flipped with nausea. Everything hurt. Muscles I didn't remember having clenched in protest.

I groaned. The sound was hoarse, ragged, as if my throat had forgotten how to make noise. My mouth was dry and my tongue felt thick.

I tried to sit up. Failed. Tried again. This time I managed a shaky elbow and dragged myself into a half-reclined position. I blinked against the brightness, squinting at my surroundings.

The space around me was dimly lit, with blinking lights somewhere in the distance, but it was enough to see that I was in a metal box. A coffin?

Panic rose, swift and sharp.

I was trapped.

Above my face was a round piece of glass, giving me a view of a high ceiling full of pipes, cables and lights. It made me think of a factory, or maybe the engine room of a ship.

The future didn't look too good. My past was shrouded in fog. All I had was the present. And in the present moment, I wanted to panic. I didn't know how I was clinging on to rational thought. This was a situation where anyone would go crazy with anxiety, right? The fact that I didn't told me something about myself: I was used to dealing with difficult situations. Or maybe I was simply brave, ridiculously brave. Either way, I was glad that I was clear-headed enough to focus.

First step, gather more information. I felt along the edges of my coffin as far as I could reach, searching for any sort of button, indentation, lever – or anything that would tell me something about my prison.

I didn't find anything beyond a few well-soldered rivets. Most of the coffin's interior was smooth, without hinges or an obvious lid. I didn't even know how this thing would open. It had to open. Right?

I pressed my face against the glass, trying to get a view of what was next to me. The room was in semi-darkness, but I could just about make out the top of a silver, curved metal ovoid next to me. I bet that's what my coffin looked like from the outside. That meant I might not be alone. And if they were awake too, they might have more information. Maybe they didn't lose their memory.

A beep sounded and the coffin shook. A click echoed through the small space.

Could I be so lucky?

With agonizing effort, I pushed the coffin's lid open. It lifted slowly, assisted by a quiet hiss of hydraulics. Cold air rushed in. I sat up all the way, swaying slightly, and planted my feet on the floor.

Running my hands down my body to search my trouser pockets, another revelation hit me. I was naked. I wasn't even wearing underwear. I shivered even though I wasn't cold. I felt exposed, vulnerable. Clothes wouldn't protect me from whatever was waiting for me.

What was I supposed to do now?

I stood. Somehow. Legs shaking, knees buckling. I braced a hand against the wall. The floor was cold beneath my bare feet. My skin felt hypersensitive, like every molecule was still waking up.

I looked around the room. None of the other metal coffins were open. Maybe I had been lucky. Or was this luck? An ominous weight settled at the bottom of my stomach. Maybe I should stay in the coffin and pretend to be asleep.

But I spotted a blinking light, next to a narrow panel in the wall. I approached it. My fingers shook as I reached out – and paused.

I was being watched.

I didn't know how I knew. But the sense crawled over my skin like electricity. Someone was watching me.

I shivered and wrapped my arms around myself. Whoever it was, they hadn't shown themselves. Yet.

Fine. Let them watch.

I was awake now.

And I would find a way out.

I touched the panel. Nothing happened. The blinking continued. This was not the exit.

My legs carried me around the perimeter of the room. I tested each panel, hoping for a seam, a lock, anything that might resemble a door. The metal was cool and seamless. The hum in the background was steady, almost soothing in a strange way. No voices. No footsteps. No hint of anyone coming.

I paused near a corner and crouched down. The floor was just as featureless up close. But something about the angle felt wrong. There was a slight dip, as if a panel could shift.

I pressed my palm against it. Nothing.

I straightened and scanned the walls again. The blinking panel drew my attention once again. Carefully, I moved back to it and tapped the surface. Then pressed my palm against it.

It flared to life, words scrolling across it in a language I didn't know. And then, before my eyes, the letters shimmered and reformed. Suddenly, I could read them.

>>WELCOME. REMAIN CALM.
ASSISTANCE WILL ARRIVE SHORTLY.
REMAIN CALM.<<

I didn't like the repetition. I didn't know if I'd like the 'assistance' that would be sent.

I wasn't sure how long I stood there, but eventually the screen dimmed again, going back to its passive state. That was fine. I had more questions than answers, but I also had time.

I wasn't afraid of the quiet anymore.

Let them come.

Whoever they were, I'd be ready.

And maybe, just maybe, someone was out there watching – not to harm me, but to help.

I let myself imagine it for a moment: a figure in the shadows, silent and waiting. A protector. A stranger who didn't feel like a stranger.

The idea shouldn't have comforted me.

But it did.

A hiss. A click. The sound of pressurisation releasing.

I spun toward the far wall, where a new panel had begun to slide open with mechanical precision. Bright light spilled in – not sterile white, but gold-tinted and almost warm. A silhouette appeared in the opening, tall and wrong and alien.

I stumbled backward.

The figure stepped into the room.

Five eyes on black fur, a tiny mouth underneath. No nose, not even nostrils. No ears that I could see among the shaggy fur. Limbs extended in unnatural directions, bending at impossible angles. The mouth opened, midnight lips around rows upon rows of tiny sharp teeth.

My breath caught in my throat.

It smiled.

"You're awake," it said, voice smooth and serpentine.

And I knew, without needing to remember, that this thing was not here to help.

It was here to break me.

To hurt me.

I didn't scream. It would have felt like admitting defeat.

Instead, I stood frozen, my bare feet rooted to the cold floor as the creature approached. My heart pounded so loudly I was sure it echoed through the chamber. I tried to breathe slowly, tried to think, but every survival instinct in me screamed: Run. Hide. Fight. Anything but stay still.

The monster didn't attack. It moved closer with eerie grace, like it had all the time in the world. The fur that covered its long limbs shimmered in the artificial light, thick and dark like a wolf's coat. Its many eyes blinked in waves, following me even as I tried not to flinch.

It stopped just short of touching distance and tilted its head.

"You're awake," it said again, as if I hadn't heard it the first time. Its voice was melodic, unnervingly smooth. Too calm.

I wrapped my arms around myself. "Where am I?"

It smiled. Its mouth was too wide, its teeth too white. "You're in Kalumbu Station. The most exclusive broadcast node in the outer galaxies."

I had no idea what that meant. I didn't care. "Why am I here?"

"To participate."

"In what?"

It didn't answer. Instead, it circled me slowly, a predator assessing prey. I turned to keep it in my sight, refusing to show fear even as my stomach knotted.

"You are unique," it said. "A mystery. No metadata, no tracking tags, no previous broadcasts. Our viewers love a wildcard."

Viewers.

Broadcasts.

Something cold and slick twisted through my gut.

"You're watching me?" I asked. "Someone's watching me?"

"Oh, darling," it said, pausing just behind me. "Everyone is."

The chill in my blood wasn't from the room anymore.

I turned. "I want answers."

It blinked all five eyes in slow succession. "You'll get them. In the Trials."

Another smile. Another wave of nausea in my gut.

"But first, I will take a closer look at you. In my quarters."

Two other monsters appeared behind it, tall and gooey and creeping-me-the-fuck-out. They bowed their heads in deference to the wolf-monster. It turned without another look, letting its lackeys deal with me.

I was along among monsters.

But there was someone else.

Someone who'd whispered to me in the dark.

And I wasn't going down without a fight.

3

VENOM

I couldn't let this progress any further. The first couple, Fay and Vruhag, had escaped the Trials with my help. Well, mostly the chii's help. I'd only done some gentle nudging, a few more sponsorships, and hacked into the Trial's security systems to allow a tractor beam to whisk them off the planet.

They were currently hiding on a spaceship, the Bloodstar, after abandoning their previous ship, the Artep, which had been crewed by a ragtag assortment of low-level criminals. For now, they were safe.

With them were the Gofren Qong and his mate, Penny. She'd turned out to be the Peritan female whose empty pod I'd found during my very first visit to the cryopod chamber. For some reason, they'd let her out and made her work as a maintenance r'hat in the sewage pipes. I'd only discovered her existence after she'd freed her mate and escaped Kalumbu Station on the Artep.

Then there was Silus, the satyr, and his human bride, Pria. Silus had been part of the Artep's crew, working as a hacker like me, but had flown to Kalumbu to save his mate. I'd given him plenty of assistance from afar, hacking into the planet's defences to open a barrier for the satyr. I couldn't resist sending him a hidden message, but I wasn't sure if he'd received it. I'd helped them again when Silus had activated an emergency beacon, disguising the signal to the space station's sensors and amplifying it for ships in orbit, namely the Bloodstar. Shortly after, letting Vruhag's shuttle onto the planet and then back into space again had almost got me caught. The station's security AI had caught on that someone was interfering with the systems and had laid a trap for me. I'd discovered it just in time, but I'd realised I couldn't be the Bloodstar's secret helper for much longer without risking mission failure.

Three Peritans had found their mates. Any moment I'd not been at work, I'd been watching their progress. They were all relatively safe on the Bloodstar.

But my mate was still here.

As were twenty-five other females still sleeping in their cryopods.

One unlucky female had been pulled from her pod yesterday and transported to the surface this morning. The thought made my coils tighten. I wanted to help her – but the longer she remained in the Trials, the longer my mate stayed untouched. Safe.

I hated that truth. I wanted to rescue them all. But I had to prioritise her.

She was my one and only.

She just didn't know it yet.

To help the female in the Trials, I had tried to get the chii involved again, but I wasn't sure if they'd received my message. If they had, they hadn't replied. Fortunately, most of my colleagues were obsessed with the Trials, so I could have them open on my screen without raising suspicion.

Still, the longer this continued, the harder it became to hide my true purpose.

And I was running out of time.

I used to think I could keep this up – split myself into two people. The cold hacker. The silent observer. But that mask was cracking. Every time I looked at her pod, I felt it slip a little further. Every time someone walked too close to the cryopod chamber, I bristled.

I was already making mistakes.

I couldn't afford more.

Because if they found out who she was to me – what she was – I wouldn't get the chance to save her.

They'd use her.

And then they'd kill her.

There was no coverage of the female just now, so I hacked into a drone and made it fly to the storage room where the pods stood. My coils tightened with every second it took for the signal to stabilise. The screen glitched, then snapped into focus.

The room was darker than usual. I switched to night-vision – and sucked in a sharp breath. I looked around the control room to make sure nobody had taken notice of my reaction, then stared at the screen again.

Her pod was open.

And empty.

My mate had gone.

Nagas' hearts are hard to stop, even with the most effective poisons and drugs, but in that moment, my hearts stopped for a click.

How could this have happened? I had multiple sub-routines running that were supposed to alert me to any mention of her pod in the system. There had been no scheduled pod opening today. And especially not hers.

I didn't know what to do. This was not planned. And I hated surprises.

Gritting my teeth so much that my fangs stabbed my lower lip, I hacked back into the system and started to write a quick programme that would search for my mate. It was a messy hack, something I wouldn't usually do, but this was an emergency. I had to know where my mate had gone. Was she already on the way to the planet's surface? She wasn't due to join the Trials for another two weeks. She was the last of the five Peritan females, I had made sure of that.

I checked on the remaining females. They were

still slumbering in their pods. Lucky them. As I was waiting for my search to have a result, I had time to write some more security protocols. If anyone got close to their pods, I would get an alert. The same should have been true for my mate's cryopod. How had someone circumvented my programme? It shouldn't be possible. I was the best hacker on Kalumbu station. Yes, there were better hackers in the galaxy, but the station's systems were firewalled from the intergalactic net. You had to be on the space station itself to access them. That's why I'd been sent here in the first place.

Someone must have erased the logs manually. A higher clearance than mine? That left only a very short list of suspects.

Fuck, fuck, fuck. My tail was trembling with anxiety and anger. No, it was more than that. Fury at myself. At my failure. If I wasn't even able to protect my mate while she was asleep, how could I ever be worthy of her?

A frustratingly gentle ping announced my programme's success. After a quick look around – all my co-workers were either watching the Trials or working – I opened the search results.

No.

Oh Glycon, no.

She was in the worst possible place in the entire station. Somewhere I could not reach her. What in the seven worlds was she doing in Jarra's quarters?

My coils constricted so tightly I had to bite back a hiss. Panic clawed at my throat, sharp and sudden.

What interest did the Prime Game Maker have in her? He hadn't paid much attention to the other Peritans – at least not until Penny and Vruhag had escaped. Maybe that was it. He might be searching for answers as to how anyone could flee the Trials. It had been impossible up to this point. Nobody ever got out of the games alive. The public thought that the few contestants who survived until the end were transported off the planet, but the truth was much darker than that.

Fuck.

I didn't know what to do. This rarely ever happened. I wasn't sure what to do with that feeling. How to cope. I wanted to go on a rampage. Slay them all. Free my mate. Kill Jarra.

But... I could not.

I remembered why I was here, why I'd signed up for this fucking job. I had lost track of that motivation over time, but now that I saw their lifeless faces flicking through my mind, I knew. It was worth it. Worth all the pretence, the waiting, the ugliness, the death. In the end, justice would be done, and I could go home.

With my mate. If I could rescue her before it was too late.

There were no cameras in Jarra's quarters that I could hack into. I wouldn't be able to fly a drone there either. I was blind.

Wait. When I'd first come to Kalumbu Station, I'd found a loophole in the code that I'd always planned to exploit, but never had a reason to. This was the perfect reason.

With the tiniest spark of newfound hope, I started typing. I kept a tight awareness of my surroundings, glancing around frequently. I was lucky that my colleagues were all captivated by today's episode of the Trials. It was a particularly bloody one. Last I'd checked, three contestants had died already.

Every room in the station had microphones installed in the ceiling, both to access the internal AI assistant and to communicate with other inhabitants. Whoever had designed the station's security systems had put a lot of effort into protecting these microphones from unwanted access, but I was not your usual hacker. I'd instinctively known I'd be able to crack the code the moment I'd looked at it. It wasn't easy and took too long – every moment my mate was with Jarra could be her last – but I persisted. The security AI was fighting me, trying to develop new lines of defence at the same time as I was writing my code. I wouldn't have long.

"...perfect. I like my contestants to have spirit."

Jarra's voice filtered through my auditory implant. I detested the male. He was a cancer that had infested not just this station, but the entire planet. Kalumbu had been beautiful once. Now it was a place of death and despair.

"Fuck you!" My mate's voice. It was the first time I heard her speak, yet she sounded so very familiar. I was glad I'd spent the past two rotations researching her language and uploading it to my internal translator. I had even learned the basics myself, just in case I couldn't fit her with an implant right away. But then the game makers had given implants to a few of the females, including my mate. Maybe that's why Jarra had chosen her. She would understand his cruel words.

"As I said. Spirit." Jarra laughed. "But now it is time for you to show me what you can do. Prove yourself and I might change my mind."

I was missing crucial parts of the conversation. What did he have to change his mind about? I hoped it was sending her down to the planet's surface as a contestant. Although...knowing Jarra, the alternative would be at least as horrible.

"Fuck you," my mate repeated.

I cheered her on mentally, yet I was also terrified of how Jarra would react. He did not appreciate insubordination and punished any misbehaviour or perceived disrespect severely. I had learned to avoid him, and if I had to interact with him, I played the perfect grunt. Jarra desired to be admired and revered. People like him were easy to handle if you knew what his needs were.

"One more time and you will suffer the consequences," Jarra warned, his voice quiet and collected, yet sharp around the edges.

This time, my mate stayed silent. As much as I didn't want her spirit to be broken, I was also glad that she hadn't given him a reason to threaten her further.

"That's better. Now we can get to know each other better."

I coiled up my tail so hard that it hurt to stop myself

from screaming. I had to do something. A hundred different options ran through my mind, none of them enough. I was ready to break my cover when K=lwr, the Quentan next to me, cursed in his native language.

"The anti-fire system is broken again. A blockage. Anyone know how to fix this without sending a r'hat through the pipes?"

A new idea blossomed. Jarra was a Irridonian. The chemicals in the automated anti-fire systems were harmless to most species, but not to Irridonians. If I could release them in his quarters, blaming the broken system, it might distract him for long enough for me to come up with a better plan.

I typed furiously, hacking faster than ever before. The anti-fire systems weren't protected much as nobody saw them as a threat to the station. Deadly if they didn't work, but nobody had assumed that they could be used as a weapon. I was a lucky bastard.

"Sorry, you will have to send a r'hat or two," I told K=lwr absentmindedly.

"Did you 'ear one of 'em escaped?" Bawwa from two workstations further budged in. "Some strange species I'd never 'eard about. Purritan or something like 'at."

They were talking about Penny. I hadn't realised her escape was public knowledge, but I couldn't worry about that now. I finished the code and deployed the hack. My coils were constricted so tight it was hard to breathe. This had to work. I didn't know what else to do.

Neither Jarra nor my mate had said anything in a

while. I checked the link. It was still live. What was he doing to her? Was she even still alive? No, she had to be. She was a valuable commodity. Jarra knew that. He was driven by base instincts most of the time, but he wasn't stupid.

A horrified scream echoed through my implant. I repressed a grim smile and resisted the urge to turn down the volume. Jarra was clearly in a lot of pain. Good. He deserved every bit of it.

"What is happening?" my mate asked in the background, sounding more curious than afraid. I was so proud of the way she conducted herself. Not surprising with her background.

Jarra groaned and screamed. My plan was working even better than expected. The Prime Game Maker was disabled for now. I had to use this time to give my mate a way to escape. I changed systems and unlocked all the doors in his quarters. As soon as I did, the sensors showed one of them opening. It had to be my mate. Without cameras, this was the only way I could monitor her progress until she was in a public corridor.

I made sure all the doors and portals on the entire floor were unlocked. Now I could-

A heavy hand landed on my shoulder.

"What the klatting rut are you doing?"

4

UNKNOWN

I was naked, shoeless, and couldn't have cared less. I ran to the door, slamming my hand against the screen on the side as I'd seen the *monster* do it. I didn't expect the door to slide open, yet it did. Thank fuck. I stumbled from the room, trying to get my bearings. I had tried to remember the way between the cargo room where I'd woken up and this place, but I'd been struggling against the two gooey monsters and had been somewhat distracted. Understatement of the century. I had been terrified. They had led me through endless corridors, pushing and shoving whenever I stumbled. There had been dozens of other monsters, leering at me, howling and growling and yipping – or maybe they weren't monsters.

Aliens.

My memory still hadn't returned but I was pretty sure that humanity hadn't encountered aliens yet. But even without my memory, I knew that I had watched science fiction films. Based on those, I couldn't help but think that this was a space station full of aliens. I hadn't spotted any other humans, which was both scary and reassuring. I didn't want anyone else to be in my predicament. Unless the other metal coffins in the first room were full of humans.

All doors opened for me. Was this a trap? Was he – if that monster was indeed male – just toying with me? Not that it mattered. I had to try and get out of here. I wasn't sure where I was running. All I knew was that I had to get away.

It had been a miracle. One moment he'd had his hands on my body, touching places he shouldn't have, the next pink mist erupted from the ceiling. It had felt cool on my skin, not unpleasant, but the monster had started screaming as if in terrible pain. I hoped he was still suffering.

His rooms had looked alien yet strangely familiar – metal chairs, cabinets, tables, a circular bed close to the floor that reminded me of a giant dog bed – but out here in the corridors there was nothing I could use for guidance. Strange symbols danced across the walls as if they were massive screens. Maybe they were. More pink mist covered the ceiling, but it was no longer filling the rooms.

I just kept running, hoping against hope that I would find a way to escape. I didn't dare think of the alternative.

Another door. On the other side were three corridors, all looking exactly the same except for the symbols flickering all over the walls. I hesitated for just a second, then took the middle corridor. It didn't matter, really.

No. I wasn't going to give up this easily. There had to be a way to escape, even if this was a space station. Maybe I could find a nice alien to give me a lift on their spaceship. Or I'd look for a spot to hide until they forgot about me.

I was being overly optimistic. Maybe that was one of my personality traits. I was still trying to piece together what kind of person I was.

A survivor.

I ran and ran. More crossroads. I always took the middle path if there was one, otherwise I went right. Earlier, there had been many monsters – aliens – about, this time I encountered nobody. I didn't have time to find that strange. My feet were freezing from running on cold metal, but I wasn't out of breath. Apparently, I was a sporty sort of woman.

I slammed my hand at yet another sensor. Nothing happened. The door stayed shut. I pushed against the screen again and again. No luck. This clearly wasn't the way.

I turned around to look for any pursuers that might be about to corner me. Nobody was coming. Yet just because I couldn't see anyone didn't mean that they weren't on their way, a few doors behind. Or maybe they were watching me. If this was indeed a place built by aliens, their technology would be way beyond anything I could imagine. There might be cameras all over the place. Maybe that's why they weren't running after me. They didn't have to. They could let me use up all my strength and then capture me once I was unable to continue.

That thought made me want to punch the wall in frustration and fear. And I did. Not punch, exactly, more of an exhausted slap.

Green lines appeared around where my hand had hit the wall, spreading rapidly, forming circles upon circles, like bubbles. They floated around for a moment, sort of beautiful, then combined into one giant circle bigger than me. The green lines flashed brightly before the wall in their centre began to shimmer. Gingerly, I touched it. But I didn't. My hand went straight through as if the wall had suddenly turned into air. Or maybe it had never been there in the first place.

I looked around one more time. The door was still locked. There were still no pursuers. I could have gone back to the last intersection and chosen a different corridor. Instead, I took a deep breath and stepped through the shimmering wall.

Warm air hit me before my eyes could adjust to the darkness on the other side. Green lines, just like the ones that had formed this doorway – or portal? – flickered across the rounded walls as if they were running away from each other. I seemed to be in some sort of giant pipe, completely dark except for the occasional flash of green lights. A row of thick black cables covered both floor and ceiling, while the walls were bare metal. It was hot and humid in here, very different from the cold corridors I'd been running through.

I peered into the darkness, trying to see the ends of the pipe. It looked exactly the same in either direction. Deep black darkness with flashing green lines racing across the walls. It didn't seem to matter which way I turned. Going right seemed like in keeping with tradition.

I'd only taken a few steps when a voice echoed through the space, seemingly coming from everywhere around me at once.

"Ssssstop. Wait there. I will come for you."

It was a male voice, lisping slightly, in an accent I couldn't place.

I froze, spinning around as if I could see who'd spoken. But of course, I didn't.

"Who are you?" I asked in a cautious whisper.

No reply. In the distance, something dripped, but the voice didn't talk to me again.

Should I do what he'd said? It hadn't been the monster from earlier. I would have recognised him anywhere. This voice hadn't sounded as creepy and threatening. But it could be a trap.

No. It *had* to be a trap.

There was nobody here to save me. Even without my memory, I knew that I was alone. Why would anyone want to help me, a human on an alien planet or space station or spaceship – whatever. It was highly unlikely. Staying here was stupid. I'd just make it easier for them to find me.

I licked my lips, realising how thirsty I was. I couldn't do anything about that.

I had to make a decision. Stay and wait or go on. It wasn't really a question. I wasn't going to become a sitting duck.

Rolling my aching shoulders, I turned right and started walking again.

The humid air felt nice against my naked skin. I was finally warm, hot even, for the first time in... who knew. I'd woken up cold in the metal coffin and had been freezing ever since. But just because I was now warm didn't mean I was any less scared. Fear drove me on, even though I was becoming markedly slower. The floor in this pipe was curved and uneven. Piles of cables and debris regularly blocked part of the way. If anyone had been in here recently, they hadn't bothered to clean up. It made me feel just a tiny bit safer from the five-eyed monster.

But had moving away from the portal been the right decision? I kept asking that myself as I walked through the semi-darkness. On reflection, that lisping voice hadn't sounded unfriendly. Or maybe it had – who was I to know what a friendly alien-monster sounded like.

The green lines flashing past me suddenly winked out of existence, leaving me in complete darkness. I stopped walking. What new terror awaited me? Had they found me? Was I about to be returned to the monster?

No. Fucking. Way.

I would fight. I would run. I would not simply give in. In his rooms, the five-eye monster had made it very clear what he intended to do to me. The pink mist had saved me – for now.

The darkness painted vivid scenes of pain and terror in my imagination. A shudder ran down my back. I had to move on before they caught me. I stumbled along, almost tripping several times. At least the pipe was entirely straight.

Something caught around my foot, and I fell. My hands hit a hill of what felt like metal wires, thin and sharp. Pain raced across my palms. I didn't need any light to know that I'd cut myself. I let myself drop back, catching my breath for a moment. My hands were burning. I pressed them against my chest, feeling warm liquid on my skin. I suppose I should be glad I hadn't fallen face first into the wires. I could have cut my throat.

Maybe I could use them as a weapon. If only the lights returned so I could see what I was doing.

As if they'd heard my wish, two single green circles appeared on the walls on either side of me, like giant eyes. Instinctively, I cowered low, making myself as small as possible.

"I told you...to stay...in place..."

His familiar voice was almost a relief.

"Glad...you moved... Change of plans. Follow the stars."

Stars?

"Who are you?" I asked, neither too loud nor too quiet.

"A... friend."

He sounded exhausted. Or maybe in pain.

"How do I know I can trust you?"

An amused hiss echoed through the pipe.

"I am... the only one...you can trust."

I hated not knowing. Was this a trick or was he really helping me?

"...have to go. Follow...sta-."

With a metallic click, his voice was gone. I was alone again.

The two green circles became smaller until they were solid dots the size of my fist. Were those the stars he'd mentioned?

They flashed simultaneously, then flitted along the walls in jagged, irregular paths. They almost seemed jumpy with excitement.

I didn't really have a choice. I got back to my feet and began to follow the dim light of the stars.

5

VENOM

I had barricaded myself into a tiny storage room, but it was only a matter of time until they broke in. The only reason why they hadn't used a blaster on the door yet was because everyone was busy dealing with Jarra. The Prime Game Maker was seriously injured and currently surrounded by an army of medical personnel, but he still found the strength to bark furious commands to find the female. *My* female. I kept listening to the transmissions from Jarra's quarters while also watching my mate's progress through the pipes. I'd not been able to give her as much help as I'd wanted, but after Briarra had caught me hacking into her uncle's security systems, I'd had to focus on my own safety for a short time. I didn't think Briarra realised that I'd been to blame for Jarra's injuries — not yet, anyway. She wasn't stupid. Eventually, she'd put two and two together. By then, I had to be gone.

Now that my mate was following my guiding stars

through the maze of waste pipes, I could take the next step, the one I'd hoped I'd be able to avoid. I had to inform my superiors. My cover was blown. I needed an urgent extraction, but I wasn't sure they would provide one. I hadn't completed my task. Yes, I had gathered highly sensitive information that would get them closer to shutting down the Trials, but was it enough? After the last data transmission, I'd been told that it wasn't. They needed yet more incriminating evidence. Although that had been before the Peritan females had been sent into the Trials. They were innocents, taken from a planet that wasn't even part of the Intergalactic Alliance, thrust into the games by force. That had to be enough.

"Come out now!" someone shouted. I ignored them and pushed my coils tighter against the door.

I typed as fast as I could. First, I started the emergency data transfer to make sure everything I'd collected since the last transmission hadn't been in vain. Next, I deployed a virus I'd written at the very beginning of my deployment to Kalumbu Station. It would wipe all trace of my presence, my work, my hacks. If I was lucky, it would work quickly enough to erase the evidence of what I'd done today. That might just save my life if the extraction didn't happen.

I hesitated before the final step. If I did this, it was all over. No way back.

I'd been desperate to leave Kalumbu for a long time now, but this wasn't how it was supposed to end. I'd failed in staying undetected and in completing my mission. If I got home – and that was a very big *if* – I would likely be demoted.

But that didn't matter as long as I had my mate with me. She was more important than any job. More important than my life, even. She was my priority.

Which is why I had to do this.

I closed my eyes and focused on a place deep in my mind that was sort of foggy, like a memory that's almost faded. I'd never had to do this in an emergency situation. During practice, it had been easy – but the last practice was at least two rotations ago. Shouts and banging against the door kept breaking my concentration.

I had to focus. Calm down completely. Difficult when you're about to be captured by the enemy.

I thought of my mate. She was relying on me to get her out of here. If I didn't help her, nobody would.

Focus.

I took a deep breath. The fog lifted somewhat. And there it was, the mind safe. It was locked securely, just as I had left it during the last practice. I entered my combination by thinking of a series of numbers, words and smells that were important to me. For a click, nothing happened. Had I forgotten the right combination?

No, thank Glycon, the safe opened, revealing the emergency comms console. I knew this was only the visual representation I had given it – for other beings, it would look very different. Not that many people were given the implant that made all this possible. It was a dangerous, unpleasant procedure, and extremely expensive at that.

I activated the console and recorded a message.

> AGENT V-29@#1 REQUESTING URGENT
> EXTRACTION FOR MYSELF AND A
> CIVILIAN. COVER BLOWN. EMERGENCY
> SITUATION. PLEASE SEND HELP
> IMMEDIATELY.

I looped the recording so that it would send continuously in the background, without me having to think about it. The implant in my brain would automatically connect to any communications equipment I was close to, hacking into it to send my message. I hoped it would reach my superiors soon.

They had always been somewhat murky when it came to extraction methods. I knew I was the only agent embedded into Kalumbu Station, so there would be no easy way to get help. They'd have to send a ship, or bribe someone locally.

That gave me an idea.

The Bloodstar was still close enough to Kalumbu to help. I had assisted them in the past, now it was time for them to return the favour. The crews' previous ship, the Artep, had docked at the station in the past, which meant their captain had the necessary clout with the criminal underworld who controlled this place. But I didn't know who was in charge of the Bloodstar and whether they were the kind of people who could enter this station. One way to find out.

I started a search for the ship's name in the security protocols. Fuck. It wasn't listed as an approved vessel.

They wouldn't let it get even close to the space station. There might be other ways for it to be of use, but it wasn't going to be an easy ride. I had to contact the Bloodstar.

For now, I still had access to all the station's systems. They'd revoke my accounts soon enough, so I had to be quick and subtle. I couldn't turn the Bloodstar into a target by directly communicating with them.

Wait, there was a new ship approaching Kalumbu. Something in the alert didn't seem right. I dived into the code, examining it from all sides. If the situation hadn't been so serious, I would have chuckled.

The ship wasn't real. It was a simulation. A good one, granted, but it was obvious once you knew. Fascinating. Who'd go through the trouble of creating a ship that didn't exist? Maybe it was a training programme designed to test the planet's alert systems. Or maybe... could it be? I examined the code in even more detail, hoping this wasn't a waste of time.

There it was.

<<<thx f0r hlp. w0rk tgth3r? B.>>>

B for Bloodstar? It had to be. They must have spotted the hidden messages I left when I helped them. Excellent. Now they could return the favour.

"Get out of there now!" Briarra called suddenly. "We have blasters trained at the door. If you don't come out, we will shoot. You'll be nothin' but stinkin' naga soup!"

Fuck. It might be a bluff – I was sure they wanted to interrogate me first to know who I worked for and how much information I'd stolen – but Briarra's uncle was wounded and she likely wasn't thinking straight.

I quickly checked on my mate again. She was still following the lights, stumbling and looking increasingly weary. I'd programmed them to lead them to an exit in a rarely used part of the station. I'd planned to meet her there. Now, that was looking increasingly unlikely.

Glycon, what was I supposed to do? Even if I contacted the Bloodstar right away, they couldn't dock at the station. The only place they could reach was the planet's surface – with my help – and that was the last place I wanted to go. I was on my own for now.

I could take on a few of Briarra's grunts. I didn't carry a weapon, but I had enough venom stored to kill five or incapacitate ten average aliens. Very few species were immune to naga venom, but there was always that chance that it might not work on one of the guards on the other side of the door. Even if I fought, spent all my venom, somehow made it out of the data centre, I wouldn't get far. I had stashes of weapons and supplies hidden away in multiple hiding places across the station, but it was unlikely I'd reach the closest one. There was no way I could shoot my way off the station.

"I'm counting to three!" Brianna shouted. "Come out now!"

Fuck, fuck, fuck. This was hopeless. I had no idea what to do.

If I got killed now, my mate would not survive.

There was no other way.

I sent a quick message to the Bloodstar, embedding it in the security protocols they were likely to monitor. I enclosed the key I used to quickly break through the planet's defences. Hopefully, they would get it.

"Two!"

I couldn't let them recapture my mate. Maybe... No, the portal was made for me. She might not survive the journey. But I had a feeling the game makers would send her to Kalumbu when they captured her. If she used my portal, at least I'd know where she'd end up. And it was a fairly safe area, if you could say that about any area in a monster-infested planet where even the plants want to kill you.

I typed two more messages, one of them to my mate with further instructions. Then I stretched, relaxed my coils, and opened the door.

6

UNKNOWN

I was desperate for sunlight. My eyes were itchy and strained from peering through the almost-darkness. The stars had led me through the labyrinth of pipes for what felt like hours. Whatever this place was, it was gigantic. Every time I expected the pipe to end, it would lead to yet another intersection. Without the stars guiding me, I would have probably ended up walking in circles.

My feet were sore. I bet I had blisters. And my mouth was drier than the Sahara Desert. The pipes seemed to be getting hotter. I wouldn't be able to continue for much longer. It was a miracle I'd managed for this long. Whatever I had been in my life before all this, I must have kept fit. Maybe I'd enjoyed going to the gym. Or maybe my job had involved exercise. My mind was still foggy where my memories should have lived. I'd almost got used to that blankness whenever I tried to access a memory.

My guiding stars suddenly flashed. I stopped walking. What the hell was going on now? If they disappeared, I doubted I'd ever find my way out of here. I'd die in a giant pipe, dehydrated, turning into a mummy never to be found.

The stars expanded, filling an entire stretch of the curved wall until it was almost bright in here. Black lines appeared on the green background, first just random squiggles, then slowly turning into letters. Maybe I should have been surprised to see English words in the Latin alphabet, but I was too curious and desperate to take much notice.

I am sorry. I tried to keep you safe and failed. They are coming. Don't resist. Don't fight. If they send you to the surface, look for the chii. Small feathered beings with multiple tails. They will look after you until I can. Continue following the stars for as long as possible. I am very sorry. Venom.

I sat on the floor and re-read the message several times. Venom, that had to be the man I'd been speaking to. A code name or his real name? I supposed it didn't matter. It was over. I'd tried to escape, but it had all been for nothing. They were coming for me, that was what he was saying. All the walking, the falls, the lack of food and water. I was much weaker than I had been when I'd escaped from the monster. Even if I went against Venom's command and fought whoever came to capture me, I didn't stand a chance.

It was over.

Except...

Continue following the stars. Was there hope? Should I continue to walk despite the thirst and blisters until my legs gave in? Where were the stars leading me? Or was it only prolonging my certain capture?

I really didn't know. And that frustrated me to no end. I needed more information so that I could make a decision. That seemed to be something that was important to me. I was learning more and more about myself. Not that it mattered if they caught me. I had a suspicion that I wouldn't stay alive for long if they did.

The message slowly faded until the green light turned back into small stars. They jumped up and down, as if impatient, and one started to move further into the dark tunnel.

I got to my feet. I wasn't going to sit here and wait. I needed to be active. Yes, it would make me even more exhausted, but I wasn't someone who would just give in like that.

Wasn't it funny how I knew exactly who I was, what I wanted and needed, but also had no idea about my past?

Putting one foot in front of the other was surprisingly difficult. My body felt heavy all over. Yet I continued on, following the stars, slowly but surely moving towards...something.

Venom's voice echoed in my mind. He and the

monster were the only two people I had memories of. I certainly didn't want to think of the five-eyed alien, so instead I focused on Venom. For some reason, I trusted him. I hadn't seen him, didn't know who or what he was, but deep inside, I knew that he was on my side. I imagined him as a man, large and tall to match his deep voice, with curly hair and massive hands. He probably looked exactly the opposite, but for now, I clung to my imaginary hero, hoping that he might yet get me to safety.

One step left, one step right, one step left...

A small eternity passed. I paused every few minutes to listen for my pursuers, but the only sound was the echo of my footsteps.

I was so focused on not tripping over the cables and detritus on the floor that I almost didn't notice that the green stars had stopped moving. They hovered on one side of the tunnel, gently pulsing like living flames. There was no intersection or even a door, just a curved wall, indistinguishable from the rest of the tunnel.

"Why did you stop?" I muttered. The sound of my voice was almost as alien to me as the real aliens-slash-monsters out there. I'd not said much since waking in that metal coffin, and every time, I'd felt estranged from that voice that was supposed to be mine. Yet another thing that I had forgotten. Or maybe my voice was simply different from what it used to be, some kind of change caused by the coffin. I didn't know and didn't really care.

The green stars pulsed more intently. I stepped

closer to the wall and ran my hands over the smooth metal, searching for hidden indentations that might suggest a doorway. Nothing.

But there had to be a reason why we'd stopped.

A bang echoed through the tunnel, followed by voices.

Fuck. They were coming for me.

I slapped my hands again the wall. "Open!" I begged. "Help me!"

The green light moved down until each star illuminated my hands. I didn't dare move. My skin itched slightly where the light touched it. Surely these guiding stars wouldn't turn on me now, at the very last moment?

The voices were coming closer. There had to be at least five or more people. Aliens. Beings. I didn't doubt for a second that they wanted me harm.

My heart hammered against my chest. I was terrified, but there was also something else in that maelstrom of emotion.

Anger. Rage.

I wasn't going to be taken back to the five-eyed monster. I hadn't come all this way only to fail.

My pinkie burned hot for a fraction of a second, then it sank through the wall. I stared at where my finger was encased by metal.

What the fuck? Two more fingers on my right hand disappeared. Then my entire hand.

Lights flashed in the distance. There was no time.

"Please let me through!" I whispered and pushed against the wall with all the strength I had left. My body burned searing hot, then I was through. I stumbled but just about caught myself. My eyes watered at the sudden influx of light. I blinked and blinked, trying to clear my vision.

I was no longer in the tunnels. I was in a goldfish bowl.

The walls in the pipe had been curved, but this room was an actual ball. I was standing in the centre of a milky-white globe about three times as tall as me. There was no furniture, no screens, nothing.

This had to be what Mr Bubbles had felt like. I felt sorry for the goldfish my parents had got me for my eighth birthday.

I sucked in a sharp breath. I'd drawn on a memory without even realising it.

An actual memory, with colours and smells and texture. I could see that goldfish bowl before my inner eye, could smell the fish food in its tub underneath, remembered the way Mr Bubbles stared at me with big judgy eyes.

A tear ran down my cheek. And it wasn't just because of the bright light.

I was becoming myself again. It was an inconsequential memory, nothing of importance, but it was only the first. Proof that my memory wasn't gone for good. Hopefully, the rest would come back soon.

As much as my returning memory elated me, I was also trapped in an alien goldfish bowl. It felt nicer in here than in the dark, grimy pipes, but this place didn't even have a door. I was just as trapped as I had been before.

I took a deep breath. I couldn't give in to despair.

"Hello?" I said quietly, just in case the walls weren't as soundproof as they looked. Of course, nobody answered. I hadn't really expected anyone to reply. I was alone. And in a horrible place like this, filled with monsters, that was actually a good thing.

"Engage portal?" a disembodied voice suddenly asked, vaguely female and just a little mechanical.

"What?"

"Portal engaged."

I sucked in a sharp breath. That couldn't be good. "No! Don't! Undo command, cancel, sto-"

I was pulled apart. My muscles stretched, strained, screamed. I was broken into pieces, screaming and crying, pain like nothing I'd ever felt, and it hurt, and I needed it to stop, and it I was going to do anything, just stop, please stop, and-

White mist clouded my vision. It was cool, moist air that surrounded me like a cloud. It erased the pain, slowly, until it was all but a memory. Of all the memories I craved, this was not one I was keen to keep.

I tried to move, my muscles aching for gentle movement after all that torture, but I was held in place by something. Maybe it was that mist, maybe it was some other force, but either way, all I could move were my eyes. The mist was too thick to see through, yet I instantly knew that I was no longer in my goldfish bowl.

Birds sang far away, leaves fluttered in a breeze, branches creaked, insects buzzed. I was somewhere in nature, outside, no longer trapped in endless dark corridors.

It's strange how you don't notice the absence of something until much later. In that bowl, there had been no smells, none at all. Here I was surrounded by them. Sweetness mixed with something like citrus. Faint notes of cinnamon and clove contrasted with heady spice. And underneath it all, earth, rain, wood. The scents were more intense than they should have been. Maybe I was more sensitive after being first in a smelly pipe and then in a place with no scents whatsoever.

A warm breeze caressed my face. I smiled without realising.

This was a good place. I was in nature, where I belonged. I spent a lot of time outdoors. I filed that as another new fact about my personality.

An earth-shattering roar broke through the bird song. Other animals screeched in panic. In the distance, a deep crack, like a tree falling.

The sounds were drowned out by my heartbeat as blood rushed to my ears. I had to run and hide. I didn't have to recognise the roar's origin to know that it was something big and dangerous.

I had to run. But I was trapped in place, unable to move, a tasty morsel waiting be devoured by an apex predator.

7

VENOM

I glared at my captors. They grinned and leered back at me. According to Briarra, I should be grateful to her that I was still alive. But I knew it wasn't out of the goodness of her heart. She was waiting for orders from her uncle, the Prime Game Maker. He may have been a relative, but she didn't dare do anything without his permission. From what I'd gathered by listening to the guards' gossip, he was still being treated by medics. My plan had been more effective that I could have hoped for. His injuries were much worse than expected. But even though I was still alive, I was also surrounded by armed goons who would like nothing more than to kill me on the spot. Finding a spy among their own hadn't gone down well. I bet some of them saw it as a personal failure to not have suspected me all along.

It wasn't their fault. For one, most hadn't been chosen for their intelligence. They were tools, hired muscle, chosen for their lack of empathy and the size of their guns. Only a few had actual skills, like my colleagues in the control room. Bawwa had come by a while ago, stared at me without a word, then left.

A small part of me would miss them. I'd spent such a long time on this station that I'd got used to the people here. None were my friends, obviously, but I'd had a few interesting conversations with some. And I had learned much by watching, observing, listening. I had built my disguise to match the station's inhabitants: a fucked-up past, a lack of perspective, no hope whatsoever, a hate of anyone remotely successful, and – most importantly – an intrinsic joy of seeing others suffer. It was sad, really, how similar everyone here was. It's how Kalumbu kept operating, rotation after rotation, built on the suffering of its contestants and the hate of its staff.

I ignored the guards and focused inwards, on that implanted communications system. My distress signal was still transmitting. There had been no reply. Not even an acknowledgement that someone, anyone, had heard me. I was on my own. And worst of all, I had no idea where my mate was. Had she followed the guiding lights to the portal? Or had they caught her before she got there?

I was pretty sure that Briarra and her followers would let me know the moment they laid hands on my mate. They wouldn't ignore an opportunity to gloat. But... wait. Did they know that she was connected to me? When they'd caught me unawares, I'd had Jarra's apartment on my screen along with a floor plan to unlock all doors and portals in the vicinity. But unless they'd managed to hack into my personal files yet – very unlikely – they didn't know that I'd been watching my female. If I played my cards right, they might think that all I did was attack Jarra, and even that was hard to prove. It would take them days to unlock the necessary data. There was a reason why I was called anytime there was an issue with the security systems. They didn't have the brains.

Silence was my best friend. As long as I didn't admit to anything, didn't offer any information whatso- ever, I might stay alive for a little while longer. And that would give me a chance to escape. There had to be a way out. This couldn't be the end.

***

"Jarra's dead," Briarra snapped. "And you will be, soon. Very soon. We're sending you to the Trials."

I wasn't surprised. A quick, easy execution on the space station was a waste for the game makers. Better to make me part of their show and let me die publicly.

"When?" I asked, keeping my expression neutral. I wouldn't give her the satisfaction.

"You're being announced to the viewers as we speak. There's never been a naga in the Trials. Want to give our audience some time to start betting. Think you'll last past sunset?"

I simply stared into her dark, cold eyes. If she was sad over her uncle's passing, she didn't show it. I wasn't sure if this made her the next Prime Game Maker, or if they would be selected from the other game makers. I didn't care. Kalumbu was a horrible place, a death trap that ate contestants alive, but I had some advantages over the poor sods thrust into the Trials. I'd been behind the scenes. I knew how it all worked. They'd make it especially hard for me, of course, but my knowledge gave me hope. I knew the geography of the planet. I knew the comparatively safe zones. And I knew the audience. If I managed to get them on my side, make them passionate about my survival, they'd bet on me. Money was power. The game makers wouldn't kill me off right away if I made them money.

Briarra was clearly disappointed in my lack of reaction. "We found the female," she said with a smirk. "I don't know if she was your accomplice or whatever, but we know you helped her escape from Jarra's room. She's on Kalumbu. And right now, she's running from a very angry prondu."

It took all my self-control not to show my emotions. A prondu. Fuck. My mate was as good as dead.

I wanted to demand that Briarra show me what was happening on Kalumbu, show me my mate, but that would give away just how much the female meant to me. Instead, I forced myself to smile at the Irridonian.

"I will miss you, Briarra. It's been a pleasure."

And I will destroy your life, I said in silence. Once my superiors acted on the data I sent them, this place would be shut down. It wasn't as much evidence as I would have liked, but hopefully it would be enough.

Wait a click. I was going to be in the Trials. An employee of the Intergalactic Authority – even though Briarra and her goons weren't aware of that – forced to participate in the deadliest games of the universe... It was the last piece of evidence. With many of the other contestants, it wasn't easy to prove that they hadn't volunteered to take part. Nobody ever got the chance to interview them before they were sent to Kalumbu. But with me, it was different.

I smiled at Briarra once more before retreating to the back of my cell. I curled my coils into tight circles and closed my eyes as if resting, then used my communications implant to send a new message.

> I DID NOT AGREE TO TAKE PART IN THE TRIALS OF KALUMBU. I WAS FORCED AGAINST MY WILL. I DID NOT GIVE CONSENT FOR THEM TO FILM ME, MAKE ME A CONTESTANT, TRANSPORT ME TO THE PLANET'S SURFACE. I AM NOT VOLUNTEERING. I AM BEING FORCED.

The sound of my cell door opening made me open my eyes. Six goons with blasters trained at me as if they expected me to resist. I knew it was pointless. Besides, they were taking me to the place I wanted to be. Kalumbu, where my mate was waiting for me. Even if she didn't know it yet.

They didn't bother tranquillising me like they did to most of the other contestants. I hadn't been given a weapon. Not that I needed one. My fangs held enough venom to kill some of the biggest monsters on the planet – if I could get close enough to bite. What worried me the most were the temperature changes on the planet's surface. If they sent me to the polar zones, I would be as good as dead. I needed warmth to survive.

But that wouldn't be good entertainment, would it? Watching a naga slowly freeze to death was no fun at all. Viewers wanted blood and violence, not drawn-out deaths by starvation and the environment. And the game makers loved introducing couples to the Trials, so there was a chance that I would be dropped close to mine. Sometimes they were existing lovers, sometimes fated mates who were yet to get to know each other. The game makers had stolen fancy tech from the Intergalactic Dating Agency that gave them the ability to test for compatibility among contestants. For some of the most promising candidates they had even commissioned space pirates to procure mates. It was disgusting.

The platform was approaching the surface quickly, heading for dense jungle. I was held in stasis, conscious but immobile, but I knew that would disappear as soon as we landed. I also knew that cameras were already trained on me. Viewers across the galaxy were watching me. If I was lucky, someone I knew back at the Authority would recognise me and send an alert to my superiors. Then they would check their communications systems to figure out why I was suddenly part of the Trials and then...

So many variables. For now, I was on my own. It fell to me to find and protect my female.

I'm coming, mate. I'm coming.

8

UNKNOWN

The beast crashed through the jungle, the noise so loud it drowned out everything else, even the sound of my ragged breathing. I was in no state to be running, my feet bleeding and my body drained of energy, but I didn't have a choice. If I stopped, I was dead. I'd only got a glimpse of the monster before my paralysis had lifted and I'd started running, but it had not looked like it was prepared to stop and negotiate. It wanted to eat me.

My only advantage was my size. I was small enough to squeeze through the dense undergrowth; the monster wasn't. It was three times as tall as me, running on two huge legs like a T-rex, with leathery wings folded against its body. I was convinced I'd seen a sharp beak protruding from its scaled head.

The trees ahead seemed to be getting ever bigger, the gaps between them tightening. Maybe I could lose the monster there. I couldn't run much longer. Already my vision was darkening around the edges. I hadn't eaten or drunk anything since I awoke. It felt like an eternity ago.

Was there even a point to continuing to fight?

Yes, every part of me screamed. Giving up now made no sense. I'd fought so hard to survive on the space station. I could fight a little bit more.

Somewhere in the back of my mind, I'd registered that I was on an alien planet, that the trees were the wrong colours, that the smells and sounds were unfamiliar, that I had no idea how far from home I was – but all that didn't matter while I was being pursued by a winged dinosaur who saw me as a delicious treat.

I reached one of the biggest trees yet, so tall I couldn't see the end of it. The lowest branches were too high above me to attempt to climb to safety. I didn't know if the monster could climb – or fly. That was a sobering thought. I needed to find a way to shake it off. Or shelter it couldn't reach.

But I had no idea how this planet worked. Were there caves? Were there areas this kind of monster avoided? Would it get tired or bored and simply abandon the hunt? Were there beasts even bigger than this one that could distract or attack it? And, most important of all, were there people? Friendly people – aliens or not – who could help me?

Because one thing was for certain: Even if I somehow survived this encounter – and that was a very big *if* – I wouldn't last long without some kind of help. I had no idea what food was edible. I'd not found a stream or river yet that would give me access to water. If that water was drinkable.

I learned something new about myself. I could think and worry even in the most taxing of circumstances. Somehow, my brain was able to separate the physical effort, the pain, the fear, from the rational part of my mind. I didn't know what that said about me. Maybe I'd been in stressful situations like this before – not that anything could be as stressful as being chased by an alien monster. That trumped everything else.

Something caught around my ankle. I was too exhausted to react in time. I crashed onto the forest floor, hard roots digging into my sore muscles. I tasted mud and blood where my jaw had hit a rock.

For a moment, I was tempted to just lie here until the monster reached me. It would be so easy to give up. Sleep, rest, die.

My vision was cloudy with exhaustion and lack of oxygen. I could close my eyes. Could stop looking at the scary world around me and pretend I was somewhere else, somewhere safe. Home.

A golden ball fell onto the ground, right next to my head. Instinct took over and I scrambled to my feet, muscles screaming in protest. I swayed as everything went black for a second or two. I blinked, knowing my eyes were open, waiting for my blood pressure to return to normal. I needed fluids.

An angry roar shook the leaves around me. It came from a different direction than I'd expected. The alien dinosaur must have been circling me, trying to find a way through the dense jungle. My strategy of running towards these trees had worked, but for how long?

Chirp, chirp.

Finally, my vision cleared, just in time to see the golden ball stretch into an animal like none I'd ever seen. Golden feathers covered it from its tufted ears down to the tips of its three tails. It was the size of a large cat, with four limbs that reminded me of the nimble arms and legs of a monkey. It stared at me with three dark, watery eyes that seemed too big for its head. There was intelligence lurking behind those eyes, and something like kindness. Pity. This was no mere animal. It was a sentient being.

I didn't know how I knew that, but I would have sworn on it with my life. This little alien was observing me not with the curiosity of an animal, but with the judgement and caution of an intelligent lifeform.

Its three tails moved behind it, swirling in hypnotising pirouettes, while the rest of its body stayed still. And it hadn't stopped staring right into my eyes.

"Hello?" I tried but felt silly right away. Of course it wouldn't understand me.

For some reason, the people on the space station – space ship? – had spoken English, although sometimes it had seemed as if their lips moved differently from the words I was hearing. I could not expect every being in the universe to also speak my language.

The little alien chittered in response without breaking its stare. It was starting to creep me out, but I didn't feel any animosity or danger from it.

The dinosaur monster roared again, sounding much closer suddenly. I was wasting time.

The feathered monkey seemed to come to the same conclusion and swirled around, its tails forming question marks above its slim body. It ran a few steps, then turned as if to see whether I was following.

I didn't hesitate. This alien being was likely to know where to hide from the monster. If I was lucky, it would show me the way.

I staggered after it, my knees weak and my head spinning. It felt like I was walking on clouds. Wherever the little alien was leading me, I hoped it was close. I wouldn't last another ten minutes.

The sound of something crashing against the trees behind us made me pull together my last remnants of energy. I would not become a monster's meal. I simply refused to. I deserved better.

The monkey-alien was faster than me. I appreciated it waiting for me every few trees. If I hadn't dragged along, it may have taken to jumping into the high branches, but with me, it stayed on the ground, always staying close to the massive purple trunks. Yes, they were purple, the colour of ripe plums. I'd stopped being amazed by that the moment the alien dinosaur had come for me, but I knew that I would need some time to simply stare and take in the *otherness* of this place at some point. Once we'd reached safety. I hoped.

Something shimmered up above, as if the air itself was glittering.

The little alien chirped in excitement and ran

faster. I struggled to even stay upright. Every step could be my last. My vision was once again fogging up. Only the hope that we might soon reach safety kept me going.

The chirping turned to something more urgent, as if it was warning me.

"I'm coming." My voice cracked, my throat painfully dry. For a fraction of a second, I imagined water, an ocean full of it, all around me, cooling my skin, running down my aching throat, providing me with energy.

Chirp, chirp.

A promise. And an encouragement. *You can do this.*

Maybe I was hallucinating, but I thought I could see an army of golden monkey-aliens running towards me. Hundreds of them.

My legs gave way beneath me. I sucked in one last breath. The sweet scent of the alien planet made me smile.

I closed my eyes and surrendered to the darkness.

I was floating in a sea of dreams. Fragments of images flashed before me, gone before I could understand what I was seeing. People of all ages, men and women, laughter, smiles, tears. I knew them and yet I didn't know who they were. Landscapes. Cities. Mountains. Oh, the mountains! I flew over crags and over glaciers, breathing in air so fresh it seemed to be newly born, far down below lush valleys and ribbons of water. Deep within my barely conscious mind, I knew that these were memories, but I couldn't make sense of them, couldn't put them in any sort of order that made sense.

Another group of people, another family. But they were different. They weren't human. Their skin was shades of green, pale spring leaves and deep ivy, their faces almost familiar, but beneath their waist, they had the bodies of giant snakes, thick scaly coils. Yet despite their otherness, I saw the same emotions as I had among the humans that I knew were my own family. Laughter. Happiness. Sadness. Love.

I smiled with true contentment. I *understood*.

Something new itched at the back of my mind. I grasped it firmly until it became part of me once more.

My name.

And I opened my eyes, fully awake, ready for life to continue.

I wasn't done yet.

9

VENOM

I was lucky. The platform dropped me in an area I knew from watching the Trials. It wasn't far from where my portal had transported my mate.

I knew it wasn't luck. It was the game makers providing their viewers with the best entertainment. They wanted me to find her. And then they wanted to see us die, in some terrible, painful way. They loved it when one of the lovers died first while the other had to watch. If the female died, the male would often go into a frenzy, able to kill monsters he wouldn't have otherwise been able to best. Not that the couples were always males and females. I had seen various pairings over the years, but the game makers seemed to prefer putting alpha males and weaker females together.

I grimaced. My female wasn't weak. She had survived an encounter with Jarra, walked almost the entire length of the space station, travelled through a barely stable portal, and was now running from a prondu. If she was still alive.

No. She was. She had to be.

I stretched my arms, rolling my shoulders. The stasis prison had made me somewhat sore, but I knew that was nothing compared to what most contestants endured before they were dropped onto the planet's surface. The game makers loved to keep them without food or water for days, weakening them on purpose.

I was in a small clearing, just about enough space for the platform to land. Around me was nothing but jungle, ancient and foreboding. The trees here had grown for millennia, their roots growing deeper than I could imagine. They blocked out most of the sunlight, but it was still warm enough for me to be at prime strength. In this part of Kalumbu, it cooled down once the sun was replaced by the light of the planet's two moons, but not enough to majorly impact me. I would be slightly slower, my reflexes dulled somewhat – but I didn't plan on spending the night out in the open. I knew the chii had a den in these woods, although I didn't know where exactly. My communication with them had always been on their terms, ever since my predecessor had introduced me to them through her secret portal. She had been the first undercover agent on the Kalumbu space station but had to retire after she'd killed an amorous guard. It had brought too much attention on her.

I would always be grateful to her for giving me access to that portal. It was how my mate had escaped the station. Not that she was in any less danger here on the surface, but at least it had got her out of reach of Jarra. I shivered at the thought of what he may have done to her if I hadn't stopped him.

I was aching to slither after my mate, but I had no idea in what direction to turn. I knew she was in this area because of the distinct colour of the trees which could only be found on this latitude, but it was still a vast distance from one end of the jungle to the other. It could take weeks to find her. Yet I knew that wasn't in the interest of the game makers. They must have deposited me within a cycle or two of my mate. If only I chose the right path.

There was no sign of any monsters, let alone a raging prondu. You couldn't miss a prondu – but you'd always hope that it missed you. I extended my forked tongue, tasting the air, searching for any trace of my mate's scent. I could sense small animals in the bushes and vines creating the thick undergrowth around the trees, but nothing larger or more dangerous than a quindibi.

Lucky. Again.

And wait, yes, underneath the layers of scents was a faint smell of a male chii. In the absence of anything better, I could follow that and see where it led. The chii had dens and burrows all over the place and they were able to communicate with each other. I still didn't know much about this mysterious species – only what they had allowed me to learn – but I was sure that they had abilities far beyond their innocent looks and demeanour. The game makers were aware of the chii in the way that predators are aware of prey too small to bother to hunt or eat. They ignored them for the most part, only ever showing them on screen by accident.

That had all changed when Fay had bonded with a two-tailed chii. I'd been too slow to change the footage, and the game makers had seen their first encounter. Questions had been asked. Nobody knew what these little beasties were up to. In the end, luckily, they had decided to ignore the incident – and I had made sure to write an AI bot that would automatically remove any chii from future footage. It was a good thing I did, or the location of one of their dens would have been revealed by a camera drone. Vruhag had destroyed the drone, but not quickly enough. Other people would have wanted some recognition for their work, but I had been undercover for long enough not to care. I'd been the Peritan females' secret guardian, and in extension, that of their mates.

Now I wished I had my own secret guardian. Would the game makers allow me a sponsor? I had been provided with no weapon, which was unusual for the Trials.

A familiar caw-caw sound ripped me from my musings. A large pink bird settled in a branch high above, watching me with interest. As was a universe of people desperate for entertainment.

I tasted the air one more time, then slithered through the waist-high grass, following the chii's scent.

With every powerful undulation of my coils, I prayed that this trace would lead me to my mate.

The scent was getting stronger. I was close to the male chii. It had made sure not to leave traces on the ground, but it couldn't hide its own distinct smell. Luckily for the chii, I was not a predator wanting to harm it. All I wanted was my mate.

I couldn't stop thinking about her. I knew she was still alive – she had to be – but had she escaped the prondu unharmed? Had she fallen prey to some other monster? And even if she had somehow evaded their notice, I knew that she was weak from lack of hydration. I'd seen the first signs while watching her in the tunnels. By now, if what I'd read about Peritan constitution was correct, she was in desperate need of sustenance. Once I found her, I would make sure to provide everything she needed.

For now, I didn't want to think about what came after our first meeting. We'd still be trapped on Kalumbu. I didn't dare hope of a quick rescue.

A camera drone whizzed past me, not even trying to stay out of sight. I glared at it. I bet Briarra was watching me, waiting for her revenge. I would make her wait. I wasn't sure how, but I would get my mate off this planet and to safety. This was not the end.

The chii's scent mixed with that of another. Then

another. Was I approaching one of their dens. That felt too easy.

Chirp, chirp!

A sound from high above made me tense my coils before I realised it was a chii. Not the one I'd been tracking, but another male. It climbed down the tree it had been sitting on, faster than my eyes could follow. From the lowest branch, still far above me, it jumped, flying gracefully through the air, before landing expertly on my shoulder. A silver chii with two bushy tails. I'd only ever seen one or two silver chii before but hadn't spent much thought on why that was.

"You are late," he chittered without greetings or introductions. Thanks to my predecessor, my translator implant had a fairly reliable knowledge of the chii language.

"Do you know where my mate is?" I asked just as brusquely.

"Yes. She needs you. We cannot communicate with her, and my Chosen has not yet arrived. She is scared, sickly and alone."

My hearts contracted painfully. "She won't be alone for much longer. Lead me to her."

The chii male didn't waste more time on talking. He simply pointed west, and I slithered as fast as I could, ignoring the scratch of the branches and stones against my scales. I hadn't been out in nature for... I didn't even know. Too long. My scales had grown soft and vulnerable. Back in the old days, on my home planet, it would not be unusual for me to spend days in the wild, hunting like my ancestors and sleeping beneath the stars. Life undercover had made me soft, at least when it came to my body.

When another camera drone buzzed closer, I told the chii, just in case his hearing wasn't as sensitive as mine.

"Follow this track," he said curtly and jumped off my shoulder, disappearing into the undergrowth. I hoped that my AI algorithms were still running, automatically erasing any traces of the chii from the footage, but I couldn't be sure. I didn't want to lead the game makers to them if I could avoid it.

I could hear the chii moving ahead of me. He hadn't mentioned how much further I had to travel. For a chii, he was especially taciturn. The chii I'd met in the past had always been chatty, full of tales and stories they desired to share. They had a rich heritage that I had only heard glimpses of, yet it had been enough to convince me that they were an ancient civilisation with a history, culture and belief system. Their small size only meant that other species underestimated them, not that they were inferior.

The first moon was already travelling across the sky by the time the chii emerged from the thicket again.

"We are here," he announced.

I surveyed the area, both for a den and yet more camera drones.

"Where are we?" I asked when I couldn't find anything that remotely resembled an entrance or burrow.

"The portal. You will have to climb this tree. We don't want witnesses, so we brought the female to our most secret den. You will be the first outsider to be granted access. If you betray us, you will die."

I had to suppress a smirk. Join the queue.

"I will not betray you as long as you don't betray me. I promise on my ancestors."

The chii sniffed, its tiny nose wrinkling. It was utterly adorable, but I made sure not to show my feelings. He was clearly a proud male.

"Do you have a name?" I asked.

"Yes. And you have not yet proven worthy to hear it."

Ouch.

I shrugged and started wrapping myself around the tree he'd pointed out, climbing as fast as I could. It was a long time since I'd last climbed a tree. I pulled myself up as far as I could reach with my arms, then curled my tail around the tree as tightly as I could, before reaching up again. It was a slow process, made harder by the sticky sap clinging to the purple bark.

I resisted the urge to ask the chii how high in the tree the portal was located. I didn't want to hear him say that I'd spend another hour rubbing my scales sore and straining muscles that hadn't seen any actions in rotations. He'd climbed past me at the very start and was waiting somewhere high above me.

When I reached the first branch stretching away from the main trunk, the chii chirped disapprovingly.

"You took your time."

I bit back a grumpy reply and simply waited for him to continue.

"You are getting close to the portal. You might want to roll up that tail of yours. I don't know what will happen if only half of you is sent through the portal."

I didn't want to find out either. I carefully made my way along the thick branch that was almost broad enough to allow for three nagas side by side. Even after watching Kalumbu on the vidscreens for so many rotations, I was not prepared for the sheer scale of this planet. Everything was oversized. The trees, the monsters, the deadliness. The chii were the only exception.

A telltale shimmer above a bend in the branch signalled the portal's location. For some reason, the game makers' drones could neither sense nor navigate the chii portals. Considering I could hear at least two of them buzzing in the distance, I was glad that we'd be rid of them in just a moment.

The chii male didn't wait. He jumped through the portal, his feathered silhouette glittering in silver light for a moment before he disappeared in a cloud of sparks. I stopped at the edge of the shimmering air and followed the chii's advice, wrapping most of my coils closely around my upper body. Moving like this was slow and difficult, but I did not want to be cut in half by the portal. With one last deep breath, I pushed myself forward and through the gateway. I was about to meet my mate.

UNKNOWN...NOT FOR MUCH LONGER

The feathered monkey chittered happily as it led me out of the cave I'd woken in. Cave seemed too poor a word for the magnificent cavern with its diamond stalactites that were reflected by the perfectly smooth surface of an underground lake. I had regained consciousness floating in that lake, the water cool yet not uncomfortably so. I'd drank my fill, then washed my aching body, always watched by a group of alien monkeys. At the edge of the water, a woven basket filled with colourful fruit and berries had waited for me. I'd forced myself to eat slowly, not knowing when I'd last had a meal. Some time before I'd been put in that metal coffin – but when had that been?

Most of my pains and aches had magically disappeared after my soak in the lake, but my head still hurt a little. It felt too full, bursting at the seams with new memories, images from another time, all shuffled together without order or structure. I'd regained my memory, but not in the way I'd imagined. It was chaos in my mind, and I knew I'd need some time to relax, sort through the memories, make some sort of sense of them. For now, I clung to the one thing I never wanted to forget again: my name.

The alien monkey chirped again and I realised I'd stopped. This kept happening. I'd been in the middle of getting dressed by wrapping a series of silky scarves around my body – provided by the alien monkeys – when I suddenly noticed I was sitting on the cave floor, a scarf in my hand, my other hand pressed to my forehead. I hoped this wasn't a permanent thing. This planet was not the place to have mental blackouts.

"Sorry, I'm coming," I muttered and continued following my guide. It was not the alien who I had met in the forest. I kind of wondered where that one had gone. Not that I was sure I'd be able to recognise it among its peers. The little aliens differed in the number of tails, size and shade of their feathers, but many of them still looked completely alike to me. Hopefully they wouldn't be offended if I got them confused.

We walked through a narrow tunnel, just tall enough for me to walk without having to crouch. It got progressively steeper, leading us up towards the surface. Behind us, other aliens chittered to each other, but they kept a clear distance. Now that I'd had both food and water, I was no longer as exhausted, but I still wanted this tunnel to come to an end. I imagined my sofa back home, a purple monstrosity I'd found in a charity shop, but oh-so-soft. You could sink into it and feel like you were floating on a cloud. I smiled. It was nice being able to remember things. Even if it was just a silly old sofa.

The walls of the tunnel were illuminated by some kind of moss that glowed turquoise, giving off just enough light to see where I was going. But it seemed to be getting lighter. And was that a slight breeze? I resisted the temptation to ask the little alien if we were almost there like a child in the back of her parents' car. Besides, I wouldn't understand their reply anyway, even if they could somehow make sense of my words.

At first, I didn't recognise the bright splotches on the walls for what they were. Sunlight. It filtered through small gaps in the tunnel's ceiling, which had turned from stone into a twisted net of roots at some point during our ascent. I hurried my steps, desperate to be outside again. But when the tunnel finally spat us out, it wasn't into the outside world. I sucked in a sharp breath and came to a stop, staring at my surroundings in sheer amazement. It was another cave, but unlike the one I'd woken up in, this one was lit by sunlight shining through its facetted, semi-translucent walls.

Walls that were made of diamonds. They were too shiny and perfect to be glass.

I was at the edge of a diamond dome as tall as a five-storey house, and I wasn't alone. Hundreds of feathered aliens were going about their business, stopping at little market stalls in the centre or jumping up and down rope ladders that led to wooden platforms above us. Their feathers were gold, silver and bronze, and their sizes varied from that of a large bunny rabbit to a Rottweiler. The aliens milling near the tunnel entrance had stopped whatever they'd been doing and were staring at me with curiosity. At least that was how I interpreted the expression in their dark, watery eyes.

A commotion on the other side of the diamond cave caught my eye. A cat-sized alien with gorgeous platinum feathers and four tails shaped like question marks made its way through the crowd, its eyes fixed on me. So far, I'd only seen aliens with two and three tails, never four. The others had stepped to the sides, forming a path for the four-tailed being. They bowed their heads in respect as it passed, before holding a fist against their foreheads in some sort of ritualistic gesture.

A sense of awe and apprehension filled me. Something was going to happen once it reached me, but what? I felt like a student waiting for their teacher to speak judgement upon their accomplishments – or lack thereof. Bronze specks glittered in the otherwise almost black eyes. It never stopped staring at me. I was being assessed, I knew that instinctively, even though I did not know the alien's purpose. The urge to run away niggled at the back of my mind, but I pushed it aside. This wasn't the time to be shy or scared. Besides, these little aliens had shown me nothing but kindness. I didn't know how they'd brought me to the underground lake, but it wouldn't have been easy. They'd saved my life. I owed them.

The four-tailed alien didn't stop in front of me like

I'd expected. It jumped up without warning, landing on my shoulder. Its tails wrapped around my arm and neck, tight against my bare skin but not uncomfortably so. For a moment, I had to fight against the irrational feeling of not getting enough air, even though the tail around my throat was the loosest of the four. Heat erupted on my skin where the feathered tails touched me. I looked at the alien and it looked *into* me.

Welcome, child, lost in time, so far from home, a melodic female voice said in my head.

Uhm... Hello. Can you hear me? Can you listen to my thoughts?

I could sense her amusement. *Only when you project them towards me. If you do not think with purpose, your thoughts remain hidden from me.*

That was reassuring. I didn't want anyone to read my mind, alien or otherwise.

My name is Sa'quii, the temporary leader of the clear-stone clan and granddaughter of Ta'quii, the great clan mother of the east.

I'm... It felt strange for a moment to have a name again. *My name is Clare. Clare Tovey from Earth. I don't suppose you know my planet? And how to get home? And how is it you can talk to me in my head?*

I wanted to ask her so many questions, but I forced myself to be patient.

More amusement filtered through our mental connection. *We are mind-linked. I have chosen you. You were tested while you were asleep and found worthy of the chii's friendship. But we shall talk more later. Your Chosen is about to arrive.*

My Chosen?

The one to heal the broken parts of your soul and make you complete once more. The one to be with you now and forever. The one who has watched over you for thousands of moon-rises and moon-sets. He is your Chosen and you are his. He is a friend of the chii and as such, we have taken steps to bring you two together faster than if we let the stars guide your steps.

Only half of that made sense. And even the bits I did understand... I wasn't sure I wanted that. I didn't need someone to heal me. I didn't need a boyfriend – if that was the kind of relationship she was describing. I was happy on my own, thank you very much. Single by choice. I remembered that. My previous relationships had always ended in disappointment. A stream of guys and girls who looked good on paper but were entirely different in reality. For the past few years, I'd used Tinder to organise the occasional encounter – I had needs, after all – but kept all emotion out of it.

It is too dangerous to be outside for the two of you. I will take you to a private cave.

Sa'quii jumped off my shoulder and walked off on all fours. Once again, the other aliens made way for her.

What are you called, your species? I asked her, immediately feeling a little rude.

We are the chii.

She led me to the other end of the cave, where a doorway was flanked by two diamond columns.

He has just stepped through the portal and is waiting for you, Sa'quii informed me.

Did you build these portals? And did you create this cave?

We did not. Beings who came long before did. But you are stalling. Go and meet your Chosen. I could hear her impatience and cringed.

I really didn't know what awaited me. Another human, brought here by aliens just like me? Or... an alien? Was he a chii?

Only one way to find out. I took a deep breath, squared my shoulders, readjusted the scarves wrapped around my body to make sure I didn't reveal parts I didn't want him to see, and stepped through the doorway.

The small room – diamond walls again that let in natural sunlight while also obscuring whatever was around these caves – was empty except for one person. He had his back to me, which I was incredibly glad for. My face had to be a mask of shock and amazement and surprise.

He was a snake. Well, half a snake. His upper body was almost human, except that his skin was covered in tiny green scales and the back of his head had growths on either side that reminded me of a cobra's hood. His arms were muscles upon muscles, with intricate moss green patterns swirling around his upper arms and back. But underneath the leather belt around his waist was a tail, as wide as his hips, curled into a heap of coils, going on and on until it ended in a fist-sized tip. If he uncoiled his tail completely, he had to be at least five metres long or more. The tail was darker than the scales on his torso, more of an emerald green that shimmered in the light.

For some reason, he seemed familiar, as if I'd seen him, or someone like him, before. But no. I could picture every single alien I'd seen as I'd been brought to the black-furred monster, and none of them had been half-snake. But why did he feel so familiar? Maybe it was my fragmented memories deceiving me. My subconscious was still trying to make sense of it all. That had to be it.

He must have been aware of my presence, but he didn't turn around. Maybe he was shy?

I looked for Sa'quii, but she had disappeared. I was alone with him. My Chosen, whatever that meant. And I really wanted to see his face. Why wasn't he turning around?

Her scent filled the room. I had trouble focusing as it overwhelmed my senses. We were finally together. We hadn't exchanged a single word yet, but this was the beginning.

I could feel her gaze on my back. I'd heard her sharp breath when she'd first laid eyes on me. She hadn't expected me to be a naga. I supposed that was fair. She wasn't used to being surrounded by aliens. Her species had barely started exploring their solar system. I had been watching her ever since the pods had been delivered to the space station. I knew exactly what she looked like, every part of her, from her delicate eyelashes to the ring-shaped scar on her right thigh. She, on the other hand, didn't even know I existed – until this moment. What had the chii told her about me?

My own chii guide had been just as rude and tight-lipped after we'd stepped through the portal and arrived in the Diamond Heights, thousands of miles from where we'd been. I hadn't known that the chii even lived here. This region of Kalumbu was rarely ever featured in the Trials. It was too remote, with too few monsters living here permanently, and radio interference from the metals in the mountains, which impaired the camera drones. It was the perfect place to hide from the game makers. I shouldn't have been surprised that the chii had chosen this area for their most secret den. Yet I hadn't expected any of the diamond hills to be *hollow*. The sunshine was refracted by the diamonds, painting the walls in all the colours of the rainbow. It was a beautiful place to finally meet my mate.

She made a strange throaty sound. My translator implant stayed silent, unable to interpret that sound.

Maybe it was time to turn around.

But I was scared. Fucking scared. What if she ran away? What if my appearance frightened, or worse, disgusted her? Nobody belonging to another species had ever described a naga as attractive. We almost always found mates among our own kind for a reason. Others mistrusted us, found us hideous.

I was a monster. She was the most beautiful female in the universe.

Fuck it. There was only one way to see her reaction. I twisted my hips, turning my torso to face her, while keeping my coils in place so I could swirl around again fast if needed.

I expected to see fear or disgust in her eyes. Instead, there was only curiosity.

That I could deal with.

"I..." My throat was suddenly dry. "I am Venom. It is an honour to finally meet you."

She smiled at me. Actually smiled. It was a small bend of her lips, without showing her teeth, but I took it as a good sign. A thin golden mark shaped like a ring wrapped around her throat. Evidence that a chii had mind-linked with her. I'd heard about this before but had never seen it in real life.

"I'm Clare." She shrugged. Inside, I celebrated that our species used the same gesture.

"You must have a lot of questions, Clare." Her name was sweet in my mouth. The first time I'd said it out loud. It was the most magnificent word in the galaxy. Clare. "I am sorry I was not there when you awoke. I watched over you while you slept, but you were woken from stasis before schedule..."

I stopped when I saw her smooth forehead contract. A sign of confusion?

"Apologies. I must start at the beginning. Am I right in assuming that Jarra did not explain where you were and why you'd been brought there?"

"Jarra?"

Fuck. She didn't even know his name. "The alien who brought you to his quarters. Furry-"

"Five eyes. Black fur." She shuddered. I wanted to take her into my arms and comfort her, burn away the memories that made her quiver. "Yes. I know who you mean."

I realised we were awkwardly standing two arm lengths apart. Behind me was a pile of living moss that the chii used as beds and seating. I pointed at it with a smile that I hoped was inviting. "Do you want to sit down? There's a lot I have to tell you."

Again, she shrugged. Her gaze wandered up and down my body, as if deciding whether I was a threat. I didn't want her to be scared of me.

"Tell you what, you sit on the moss, I will make myself comfortable here. Nagas don't really need chairs."

"Nagas?" she asked as soon as she'd taken a seat. Her back was upright, her hands clutching her knees. It was obvious she was ready to jump up the moment she felt threatened. I cursed Jarra and the game makers. It was their fault she'd been in danger, that she was so suspicious of me now. But we were talking. And there had been smiles. I should be grateful for that.

"My species," I explained. "We originate on the planet Serpenthyra, but I have lived on space stations and ships most of my adult life. I will tell you more about us, but not now. We should focus on the current situation."

She nodded. "That seems like a good idea. Give it to me. Why am I here?"

Such a simple question with such a complicated answer. Instinct made me want to protect her from the truth, but she had to know.

"We are on a planet called Kalumbu, but you were first woken from stasis on the station orbiting the planet. How you got there... I managed to piece most of it together, but there are gaps. Somehow, you ended up on a slave ship. I assume the slavers came to your planet and abducted you, or maybe someone else did and sold you to them. That slave ship was attacked by pirates, who took you – well, the stasis pods you were kept in – to an auction, where one of the game makers acquired you. They had you transported to Kalumbu Station."

I observed her closely to make sure she was processing my story. So far, she seemed to be doing alright. She'd cringed at the mention of slavers and pirates, but didn't interrupt.

"This planet is not like any others. The chii are the only sentient civilisation that live here, and most people don't even know about them. This planet is ruled by the game makers. They send contestants down here along with the most terrifying monsters from across the galaxy. It's called the Trials of Kalumbu and it's big business. Gazillions of people watch it all around the universe – it's not legal, of course, but that doesn't matter. Contestants rarely survive. It's a fight to the death. And-"

"Wait. I didn't sign up for this. How can they enter me into these games if it wasn't my choice?"

A cold laugh escaped me. She shrank back, and I regretted it instantly.

"Viewers think that contestants are here voluntarily, but that is a lie. They have no choice. Neither do the monsters, to be fair. Both are transported onto this planet by the game makers – and everything is filmed. The more bloody and brutal the deaths, the higher the viewing figures, the more money they make. It's simple." I sighed. "I am sorry to be so blunt, but you deserve to know."

She pushed her shoulders back and stared at me defiantly. I was so very proud of her in that moment.

"I am grateful. You are right. I deserve to know. I need to know. It's hard to make decisions if you don't have all the information. Are you a contestant, too? No, wait. You said something about watching me sleep, and you sent those stars in the tunnels, right, so you must be... No. Do you work for them?"

Fuck. I'd dreaded that question.

"No... It's more complicated than that. I was sent here as a contestant, just like you, but until the moment they caught me, I was working undercover on Kalumbu Station. I was tasked by the Intergalactic Authority to infiltrate the space station in order to gather evidence. The IA want to shut them down, but all previous attempts have failed. The game makers have too much money and influence. This time, the IA played a long, secret game. Unfortunately, I was discovered while helping you escape from Jarra's clutches."

"That sprinkler system that burnt his skin, that was you?"

"Yes. It was not the best solution, and I am sorry that it took so long to implement, but I had no time to prepare. I didn't realise he'd woken you from your stasis pod until it was too late. There were supposed to be other Peritans before you-"

"Peritans?"

"That's what your species is called in Intergalactic Standard. You prefer... humans, was it?"

"Yes. Human. Who came up with Peritan? I don't think any Earth language calls us that."

"I don't know. I read up on your species as much as I could, but there is not much information available. Luckily, I found language files for my translator implant, which is why we can communicate easily. Although that was before the game makers fitted you with an implant yourself."

"An implant? What the fuck? Where?"

She grasped her head, her delicate fingers searching for scars. Sadness filled me at the sight. She'd never had a choice. Ever since she'd been taken from her home world, she'd been treated as a voiceless animal.

"It's in your brain," I said softly. "There won't be a scar."

Her eyes were wide with anger and fear. "What else did they do to me?"

"There is a tracker implant near the top of your spine, but while I was still on the station, I disabled the link to it. Unless the game makers find a very talented hacker, they can't track you. At least not for a while. This chii den lies in the Diamond Heights, an area the game makers rarely ever send contestants to. The camera drones don't work here, and since our suffering is their entertainment, they don't see the point in using this part of the planet for the Trials."

She sighed deeply. "That is somewhat reassuring, I suppose. I have so many other questions, but I don't know where to start. I guess I understand now how I came to be in this place, but I still don't know who you really are."

"I'm an undercover-"

"That's not what I mean," she interrupted. "What are you to me? Why did you help me? Why did you watch me while I was in that metal... stasis pod, is that what you called it? And why did Sa'quii call you my Chosen?"

Ah. And I'd thought explaining the Trials was diffi-cult. This would be even tougher. Should I ease her in gently or drop her right into it? So far, she had stayed remarkably calm and collected. She was just as intelli-gent as I had expected from reading her file.

"Please, just tell me."

I tightened my coils as my hearts drummed in my chest. "The chii call you my Chosen, but you... you are my mate."

"Mate? As in friend?"

She seemed very relaxed now. Not the reaction I'd expected.

"No. Not as in friend. I mean, I want to be your friend, but also so much more. You are my mate, my *soul*mate. Our souls have been searching for each other from the moment we were born, calling from across the galaxy. We are meant to be together, Clare. Now and always."

12

CLARE

I was speechless. And now that I had most of my memories back, I knew that this was an unusual occurrence.

Had this guy – this *naga* – just proposed to me?

I felt a little queasy, as if I wasn't quite in my body anymore. If this was a dream, it was high time I woke up.

"Are you alright?" he asked cautiously. His eyes were somewhere between snake and human, with a slitted pupil surrounded by warm shades of brown. He had no lashes, but there was a dark line around his edges. Unless he'd gone through the effort of applying eyeliner before being sent to this torture planet, it had to be a natural marking.

I realised I'd been staring into his eyes for a little too long. My cheeks heated with embarrassment. He may have been an alien, but that didn't give me the right to stare at him like an exotic animal. As much as he fascinated me, I had to stay rational.

"I don't know," I said, surprised at my honesty. "I really don't know. My brain is still grappling with the fact that I'm on an alien planet and that aliens are watching me for their entertainment. It's sick. And then there's you... It's too much. I can't process this. Why did you say that? This...mate thing."

He looked at me with sad puppy eyes. "Because it is true," he said, lisping slightly, probably due to his forked tongue. I swallowed hard. His *forked* tongue. "But you are right. It is a lot to take in. I should not have overwhelmed you with so much information at once. Shall we... I propose we go back a bit. Let's figure out how we get off this planet first." It was obvious that he was not happy with that decision, but I was glad he'd found a compromise.

"Can you take me back home?" I asked. "How far from Earth are we?"

That sentence felt very strange. I was used to thinking in small distances, the bus journey between my home and work, the two-hour flight to see my auntie in Switzerland. Using *planets* as my point of reference was a new thing altogether.

He didn't answer right away. Then... "Yes. Probably. I don't have a spaceship myself, but I have enough credits saved to hire one. Or the Bloodstar might be able to help out. But let's discuss that once we've actually made it to safety. We are safe for now with the chii, but as we speak, the game makers will be wondering where we've disappeared to. If we were normal contestants, they might wait and see for a while in the hope that one of the drones will track us. But we are not. I killed Jarra, the Prime Game Maker, and they will see you as somehow involved in his demise. They want us to suffer. My former supervisor, Briarra, is the vengeful kind. She will stop at nothing to make sure that I die a brutal, horrible death."

My heart sank as I listened to him. This did not sound like we stood much of a chance at all. But I wasn't prepared to die. Not after all that had happened. I was more prepared than ever to do whatever it took to survive.

"What do we do? How do we leave this planet before they can find us?"

"There is a spaceship, the Bloodstar. Three other Peritan...human women and their mates are on that ship. It is a long story, and I will tell it to you some time, but not now. Safe to say, they have a vested interest in rescuing you and the remaining females from the station. What I need to figure out is how to get in contact with them. The chii don't have their own technology; they rely on relics and artifacts from times long gone, left by a civilisation whose name has been forgotten. I doubt they will have the ability to contact a spaceship through the virtual barriers in place around the planet."

Something had niggled at the back of my mind while he'd spoken. "You mentioned other human women. How many of us are there?"

"Thirty pods arrived on the station. Three females sadly died. One, Penny, woke up early and became a slave until she met her mate and escaped. Two others, Fay and Pria, were sent to the Trials, but again they managed to escape along with their mates. One other, a female called Hazel, is somewhere on this planet, but she was sent here while I was trying to save you from Jarra's clutches, and I don't know what happened to her. The other twenty-two are still sleeping in their cryopods on Kalumbu Station."

"We have to save them," I said immediately.

Venom gave me a small smile. "I agree. But we cannot help them while we are trapped on this planet ourselves. We need allies and we need resources. Just before I was sent to the surface, I sent a distress call to the Intergalactic Authority. If we are lucky, they will mount a rescue operation – but it's unlikely. They have no resources in the area, as far as I know. It would take them too long to reach Kalumbu. By the time they'd get here, we will be dead. For now, the crew of the Bloodstar are our best hope. I sent them a message just before I was captured. If we're lucky, they will have received and deciphered it by now."

I could see he was trying to give me hope, but he didn't seem entirely convinced by his own words. There were a lot of 'ifs'. A lot of luck. I preferred to make my own luck. I didn't like to rely on other people.

"What can we do ourselves?" I asked. "I'm not going to sit here and wait for a rescue that might never come. What if we're stuck here forever? Can we live with the chii?"

"No. The game makers would find us eventually. They would not be kind to the chii for harbouring us. I don't want to put the chii in danger more than I already have. But we should talk to them. They are intelligent and wise, more so than they appear at first sight. I believe they have survived for this long by pretending to be prey animals, driven by instinct rather than sentient thought. That makes it easy for the game makers to ignore them."

I had to admit that when I'd first seen the chii that had led me here, I'd assumed it was just an animal. Only the intense look in its eyes had given away its intelligence.

"Then let's talk to them," I said, getting up from the mossy heap. "As much as I have about a thousand other questions that need answers, I also don't want to sit here all day if that delay could mean we'll be in danger later on."

Venom inclined his head, his expression serious. "You are right, mate. We shall talk to the clan mother."

Sa'quii and a silver chii with two tails, slightly bigger than her and looking decidedly grumpy, were waiting in the main cave. They were having an animated discussion, chittering loudly, but stopped when Venom and I approached. I wasn't sure what word to use for how Venom moved. It definitely wasn't walking. His lower body moved in a slithering motion, while his torso stayed upright, his eyes fixed on me. He smiled when he noticed me staring at him.

Sa'quii grabbed one of the silver chii's tails and held it towards Venom. *My idiot Chosen just admitted to me that he hasn't mind-linked to you yet, naga. Until he does so, he cannot talk to your female. She does not speak our language like you do.*

Just like before, I heard her voice in my head, but this time, she was also chirping in her birdlike language for Venom's sake. I looked at Venom in surprise. He could understand their language? He rose a little in my estimation until I remembered the translation implants. Maybe his could translate the chii's language while mine couldn't.

Venom's eyes widened at her words. "He is your Chosen?" He sounded dubious.

Sa'quii chuckled. *He can be a little rough around the edges. He grew up far from civilization and is still learning manners. I apologise if his behaviour offended you.*

"I am not offended," Venom said quickly. "I just hadn't realised that the chii who led me here was the Chosen of a clan mother."

I am not a clan mother. I lead the clear-stone clan only while our clan mother is absent, but as soon as she returns, I will return to my previous rank. I am not worthy of leadership.

The other chii chirped something which sounded like a protest or argument.

Sa'quii exposed her fangs at him. They were dangerously sharp. He hesitated for a second, then presented his throat in deference.

Ba'quoo will link to you now, naga, if you agree.

I wanted to know more about the situation, but I stayed quiet. This mind-link was the reason I could understand Sa'quii, so I supposed there wasn't any harm in it. What I didn't understand was why Venom needed it when he could speak their language.

Ba'quoo pulled his tail from Sa'quii's grip before jumping on Venom's shoulder in one huge, elegant leap. He wrapped his tails around the naga's neck, just like Sa'quii had done with me. He chirped something at Venom.

"I understand and I agree," the naga muttered, his attention fully focused on the chii.

Something passed between them that I couldn't quite describe. A sort of energy. It was over in a just a few seconds. The chii jumped down to the diamond floor again, taking his place next to Sa'quii. She entwined one of her tails with his and smiled at him with pride.

I turned back to Venom – and gasped. A golden mark had appeared on his scales, right where Ba'quoo's tails had been wrapped around his throat.

"What is that?" I exclaimed before I could stop myself.

A sign of their mind-link, Sa'quii explained. *You*

have one as well. It will fade while we are together and appear when we are apart. If you touch it and think of me, it will guide you to wherever I am, no matter how far.

I tried to look for the mark, but it had to be around my neck where I couldn't see it. I wished they had a mirror. The diamond walls of the cave only refracted the sunlight coming from outside, but didn't offer a reflection.

"Will it ever go away?" I asked aloud before I remembered that we could talk in our minds.

If you want it to. She sounded almost offended. *This mind-link relies on both of us to stay active.*

A commotion at the other end of the cave made us all swirl around. From the corner of my eye, I saw that Venom had moved ever so slightly closer to me, as if trying to protect me from whatever was happening. I found that surprisingly sweet, even though I was used to looking out for myself. Growing up on a council estate in a rough part of London will do that to you.

A tiny chii, the size of a bunny rabbit and with only one golden tail, ran up to Sa'quii.

It stood up on its hind legs and chittered wildly.

"A flying eye has been spotted," Venom translated for me. "A drone. They have found us."

13

VENOM

I wanted to wrap my body around her, protect her from what was to come. I was so very tempted. But I resisted the urge, tensed my muscles and tried to focus on what was being said. I hadn't expected the game makers to find us this quickly. Maybe they had managed to re-activate my mate's tracker faster than I'd thought possible. Or they had sent a drone through a portal, even though that should short-circuit any drone that attempted it. How ever they had figured out that we were in the Diamond Heights, it was bad news for us. And for the chii.

I rubbed my neck where I assumed I now sported a mark similar to my mate's. I could just about feel the presence of Ba'quoo's mind when I focused on the chii that I mind-linked to. I'd never expected that I would be given this great honour. I'd interacted with the chii ever since I'd taken my posting on Kalumbu Station and had been introduced to them by my predecessor, but all communication had been short and to the point. I'd helped them by hiding them on the Trials feeds and they had in return provided me with information about what was happening on the planet's surface. I'd come to admire them for their tenacity and strength. Now, I would have to rely on those qualities.

We will have to – I began in my mind, testing the connection. *Ma...Clare, can you hear me? Is this working?*

I can hear you. She sounded somewhat confused. *How can I hear you? We're not mind-linked, are we?*

Sa'quii *pulled* on the connection to signal that she was next to speak. Apparently, there was an etiquette to this mind-speak.

You are linked with me and Venom is linked with Ba'quoo, who is my Chosen. If he did not share this bond with me, you two would not be able to talk to each other.

I had questions about the capabilities of this bond, seeing the potential advantage it might give us in our fight against the game makers, but there was no time.

We have to leave, I announced. *We will not put you all at risk. Clare and I have to show ourselves to the drone before the game makers decide to attack this place in order to flush us out.*

They cannot see us from the outside, Ba'quoo interjected. *We are hidden from view. The diamonds twist the light, letting it into the mountain but disguising us from the outside world.*

No, they know we're here. How often do you have a random drone in this area? Exactly. Somehow, they tracked us. It is better if Clare and I leave. Immediately. I very much appreciate your help so far, but I don't want to endanger you any more than we already have.

I agree, Clare said. *But where can we go? Is there anywhere that's safe?*

I suppressed a cold laugh. No, there wasn't. This planet was created to be a death trap. But I couldn't say that to my mate. I wanted her to hope.

Ba'quoo chirped excitedly. *There is another cave, one that the Big Ones used a long time ago. They have not been there in generations. I can lead you there. It is far enough from this den to offer safety to the other chii, yet you should be able to reach it just after sunset.*

Fuck. Sunset. The portal had taken me to a different part of the planet, far further to the north than my previous position. It got cold here at night. Cold enough to pose danger to a naga. But we also couldn't stay here. And even if we took the portal back, the camera drones were probably scanning that area as well.

There was nowhere to hide on Kalumbu.

Our only hope was to delay our capture long enough for help to arrive. If there was any help to hope for.

I zoned out for a click to check on my communications implant. No response, but it was still transmitting. Wait. What if this was how the game makers had tracked us to the Diamond Heights? Unlikely, highly unlikely. But better safe than sorry. I turned off the broadcast but kept a channel live to receive any potential message. If we evaded the drones again and they didn't manage to find us a third time, it would be proof that my implant could be tracked. How ironic would that be.

"Everything okay?" my mate asked aloud. I must have looked strange, unmoving, my gaze focused inwards.

"Yes. Sorry. We should leave soon." I switched back to mental communication. *Ba'quoo, Sa'quii, could we get some supplies from you? Food, water, blankets, any kind of weapons you may possess?*

We do not use weapons, Sa'quii said dismissively, almost sounding offended at the thought. *But we do sometimes collect what we find in the jungle. Big Ones drop them carelessly. Ba'quoo will take you to our storage cave, while I will have a little chat with Clare. There are some things she needs to know.*

I was tempted to ask what those things were, and whether we really had time for that, but I knew better than to argue with the leader of the chii. Despite her size, she was a formidable character. I was almost a little scared of her.

By the time we left the diamond cave, the first moon was high in the sky and the second had broken past the horizon. The sun was edging towards the mountain range in the east. We didn't have much time left. The temperature already seemed lower than when I'd arrived.

I searched the skies for the drone.

Ba'quoo pointed south. *It is flying somewhere there. Do you want to attract its attention?*

It was exactly the opposite of what I *wanted* to do, but it was necessary for the chiis' protection. As long as the drone was searching for my mate and I, the chii were in danger.

I sighed grimly. *Yes. But you should be gone by the time it gets here. Can you point us towards the other cave?*

Ba'quoo chittered with irritation. *Why did I get matched with the stupid one? I don't have to be with you to guide you. The other cave is within mind-speak range. I will tell you where to go from the safety of my den.*

To my surprise, my mate chuckled. Was she amused on my behalf? Making fun of me?

I had to be better. Smarter. Impress her so she would no longer doubt that we were mates. I had to be the best naga I could be. If only I could have focused completely on my mate rather than surviving on a hostile planet.

"Then let's go," I said aloud. "Give us a few clicks to get away from the cave entrance, then I will make some noise for the drone's sensors."

Ba'quoo swiped his tails against my scales, as if to say goodbye or wish us luck, then jumped off. Other chii who had been watching us curiously also disappeared into the mountain's heart. I really hoped we hadn't endangered them with our presence. This was their safe haven, far from monsters and the Trials.

"It's just us now," Clare said with a brave smile. "Do you think the other cave will be as beautiful as the one we just left?"

"If it's also made of diamonds, that is likely. But I don't know what the chii meant when they said that 'Big Ones' used the cave. If that's to say that the game makers used it, we might not be as safe there as I'd like us to be."

I tightened the straps of the makeshift backpack containing our supplies. Ba'quoo had also given me an ancient axe that needed sharpening but would do for now. My mate, insisting that she could carry something, held our blankets. Even that had been a struggle for me to allow. The chii had told me what she had been through. The waters deep within the mountain had healing properties, so they'd said, but even after spending hours floating in there, Clare wasn't fully recovered. She hid it well, but sometimes she would wince when her leather-wrapped feet stepped on a rock.

We walked in silence, following a narrow path through the rocks that gently climbed past massive boulders. Around us, the diamond mountains reflected the fading sunlight. The peaks reached high into the sky, far past the clouds, forming a sharp ring all around us. We were in a valley, yet even this had to be at quite some altitude, much higher than the jungle. Sadly,

Clare and I would be affected by the altitude before the drones were.

When we were a fair distance from the chii's hide-out, I made Clare stop. We had reached a small plateau that opened up the most magnificent views across the Diamond Heights. I wished we could stay here for a while, enjoy the scenery, maybe have a romantic picnic. Instead, we had to call the enemy to us. How ironic that I was about to purposely endanger our safety.

"It is time," I told my mate. "I will attract the drone's attention. Once it has us tagged, it will stay with us, observing us every click of the day. I very much hope that the cave we are going to has a small enough entrance that we'll have at least some privacy from the game makers."

"Can the drone harm us?" Clare asked with a worried frown.

"No. They have no offensive capabilities. If they're attacked by the local fauna, they can emit a sonic wave to stun beasts for just long enough to get out of their reach, but otherwise, they are built to observe only."

"Good. I mean, not good, I'd rather we didn't have anyone watch us, but I understand it's necessary. Goodbye privacy, I guess."

"Goodbye privacy," I echoed grimly.

I picked up the biggest rock I could safely lift and slammed it against a diamond pillar to my right. The pillar was fine – the rock wasn't. It shattered with a bang, echoed by the mountains around us. I did it again, and a third time, until I picked up the telltale buzz of the drone.

"It is coming," I warned Clare. "From now on, don't mention the chii." *At least not aloud. We can speak about important things telepathically.*

I was even more grateful to the chii now for giving us access to this ability. It would give us a major advantage that the game makers wouldn't anticipate.

When I saw the drone in the distance, its sleek metal reflecting the light of the setting sun, I motioned for Clare to continue walking. I let her set the pace, but we were evenly matched. The path was mostly smooth, but occasionally a sharp rock would scratch against my scales. Nagas were not made for this environment. I could already feel the air cooling. Diamonds did not store heat like other rocks, that was very obvious to me now. We had to reach this other cave as fast as possible.

"It will be dark soon," I said into the silence. "Are you able to walk a little faster? I read Peritans don't have good night vision, and I don't want you to stumble in the dark."

She increased her pace somewhat. I grit my teeth, my fangs digging into my lower lip. I didn't want my mate to have to exhaust herself, yet we had to get to safety. My entire body ached from the climb and I felt myself getting slower. The cold was sucking all the energy from my muscles.

The drone was close now, but kept a small distance from us, as if the game makers were worried we'd attack it. They knew drones could be destroyed. Contestants did it all the time. A well-aimed rock, a bang with a tree branch, a slice with a blade. In other areas of the planet, drones were numerous and easy to replace. Here, this had to be the only one. I still needed to figure out how it had found us so quickly. Our lives depended on it.

I was out of breath by the time the path widened slightly before turning into another plateau nestled against a huge rockface. A crack shaped like a lightning bolt went all the way from the top of the rock down to where we stood. What could do this to solid rock?

This must be it, I said in my mind, unwilling to let the drone eavesdrop on us. *Let's hope the cave hasn't collapsed.*

Clare looked at me with dread, and I instantly regretted voicing my fears. Her gaze flitted to the drone hovering high above us, before settling back on me. Warmth spread through me; warmth that did not come from the sun. I smiled at my mate. This was not how I'd imagined meeting her, but I was grateful that we were finally together.

An icy breeze caressed my scales. I could feel the cold seep into my body. I had to find shelter before I became unable to move.

We approached the crack in the rock face. In the fading light, it appeared dark, black almost, as if someone had dipped a paintbrush into midnight itself and carelessly struck the rock with it. But at the bottom, where it met the smooth ground, something sparkled. Another diamond?

Clare bent down to look at it.

"It's a-" She stopped, then continued in my mind. *It's a key. At least I think so.*

She handed me a tiny diamond obelisk, about the length of my finger. A delicate pattern had been engraved into it on all sides. It reminded me of a web that had been spun around the diamond. Beautiful. But why did my mate think this was a key?

I asked her the question. She grinned.

Because there is a hole in the rock. Look here. I think this will fit.

I handed the obelisk back to her. *You found it. You deserve the honour of opening the door. If it is one.*

She took it from me, her delicate fingers brushing against my scales. Our first touch, no matter how small. Something moved deep inside me. Something that had lain dormant all my life. I froze. I should have expected this. She was my mate, after all. But for all the stories I had heard, for all they had taught us in school, I had not expected it to feel this *good.*

Fingers crossed, my mate said, oblivious to what was going on inside me. *Let's see if this works.*

I wasn't sure why she needed to cross her fingers at this moment in time, but there was no time to ask. She pushed the obelisk into the hole. For a moment, nothing happened.

Then the mountain groaned, slowly waking from an age-old sleep.

14

CLARE

The rock in front of me vanished.

I blinked, not believing my eyes. One second it was there: solid, grey stone that had felt as hard as any rock would. The next second, it had disappeared, revealing a dark tunnel entrance. I tentatively stretched out my arm to feel for the rock that had been there. All my fingers found was air. The rock really had vanished. Wow.

"That was...unexpected," Venom said from behind me. His voice shook slightly. Exhaustion, maybe? It couldn't have been easy to move up this mountain without legs. He had an effective slithering motion that enabled him to keep up with me, but I'd seen him wince whenever a sharp rock had touched his scales. Not that I'd been walking particularly fast. My feet had miraculously healed from most of my injuries, but I was still sore and exhausted. Would a comfortable bed be too much to hope for in this cave?

I turned to look at the drone that had been following us at a steady distance ever since Venom had first attracted its attention. I'd got used to the slight whizzing sound, although I refused to think about what it symbolised. People were watching us. They knew where we were. And they did not have our best interests at heart.

Hopefully, it wouldn't be able to follow us inside. The gap in the rock was just about wide enough to allow Venom to squeeze through.

Ready? I asked in my head. I was getting more and more used to our telepathic communication. Not that we'd talked much on the climb up here. We'd both needed all our focus for the narrow, rocky path.

Let's find out what awaits us. I will go in first.

I wanted to argue with that, but Venom knew more about this place, this *world*, than I did. It made sense for him to lead. But I made a mental note to remind him in future that I was not going to stand behind him at any sign of danger. I was a strong, independent woman. I'd known that even before my memories had been returned to me.

He squeezed through the opening. I couldn't resist watching how elegantly he moved. He was so very alien, yet familiar at the same time. He was strong yet flexible, snake-like yet also human. My gaze flitted downward. He did not have a bum, not like a human would. And while the leather belt covered where his crotch would have been, I was sure he did not have anything...hanging there. I tried not to blush as I imagined how nagas made love. I was fascinated by him and desperate to find out more about his kind. But I also knew that we had to focus on surviving in this hostile world. I remembered the dinosaur-monster that had been chasing me and shuddered. Just because there weren't any monsters right now didn't mean that we were safe. All we could hope for was that this cave wasn't already occupied by something hungry.

"Unbelievable!" Venom exclaimed suddenly. With one last look at the diamond mountains painted orange by the setting sun, I followed him into the cave.

A short, dark passage barely gave way to the unexpected. I suppressed a gasp as I joined Venom who was waiting for me on a stone ledge. A huge cavern lay before us, bigger than the chii's den, bigger than any I'd ever seen. The ceiling was mostly made from a smooth, black rock, with small patches of diamonds that let in some light. Glowing orbs attached to the walls gave extra light. The floor was covered in crates of all shapes and sizes, ranging from something small enough for me to carry all the way to metal boxes as tall as a house. To our right, a dark tunnel entrance loomed. This cave may not be the only one beneath this mountain. A cool draft made me shiver.

"What are all those crates?" I asked Venom.

"See that logo on the big one over there? That's the original Trials of Kalumbu emblem, from back when the game makers first started broadcasting. That was many generations ago. I wonder if they did not have the same facilities in orbit back then and relied on having places for storage and supplies on the planet's surface."

"Is this safe? If this cave belongs to the game makers, won't they have cameras in here, or some other surveillance system?"

"I doubt anyone remembers this place," Venom said thoughtfully. "I certainly never heard about it, and I have been deep in the Kalumbu systems and archives. There are a few small outposts scattered about the planet, mostly for drone maintenance and repair, but nothing as big as this. We will proceed with caution, but I don't think we are in any immediate danger."

I still didn't feel comfortable with the situation. "But they know where we are now. The drone is still outside."

Venom looked at me, exhaustion suddenly evident in his slouched shoulders and half-closed eyes. "Yes, they do. But remember, this is a game for them. We are their entertainment. They won't send some of their goons to kill us in our sleep. They want our deaths to be graphic and brutal. They will flush us out until their monsters can do their dirty work. For tonight, we are safe. I promise."

I wanted to argue that there was no way he could promise me such a thing, but I was tired as well. Maybe it was better to keep up the illusion of relative safety. And staying in this cave was miles better than sleeping outside.

A narrow ramp led down from the ledge to the cave

floor. I was starting to suspect that we'd come through some kind of emergency exit and that the cave had a larger entrance somewhere else. These crates had to have been brought in somehow. Hopefully, that other entrance was locked and wouldn't let in any monsters.

It was markedly colder in here than in the chii den. "What are the chances we might find some warm clothes and cushions in those crates?" I asked, trying to sound upbeat even as a shiver ran down my arms.

Venom grimaced. "Very unlikely, I'd say. But at least we have blankets. Let's find a comfortable spot, then we can explore the cave further."

This time, I took the lead, even though I could see Venom wasn't too pleased by that. He just had to get used to the idea that I was not going to cower behind him like a damsel in distress.

The cave floor was so smooth that I almost slipped. The leather wraps the chii had provided me with had protected me from injuring my feet during our hike, but they were slowly unravelling. They were not a long-term solution, but I doubted I'd find shoes in any of the crates. It was strange how you didn't appreciate simple things like shoes and clothes until they were taken from you.

The gaps between the crates were large enough for Venom and me to walk side by side. Well, I walked, Venom slithered. His movements were becoming slower. Was it just exhaustion or something else? His stoic, determined expression made me keep quiet and resist the urge to ask him if he was alright.

"Look, over there!" He pointed at a huge stack of crates to our left, right underneath a diamond patch. "That crate is open. Shall we have a peek?"

"Definitely. I'd quite like to know what they're storing in here. If you could wish for anything you'd wanted, what would you like to find in the crate?"

Venom chuckled. "I like this game. But my wish has already been answered. You are here with me."

I swallowed hard as heat pulsed through my body. I should laugh it off, but I was really touched by his words. They were cheesy, but they were also resonating deep within me. Did I really mean that much to him? When we'd only just met?

"I apologise, I should not have said that," he muttered, misinterpreting my silence. "I will keep to our arrangement and focus on our survival."

Venom turned to the open crate which reached to his scaled chest. Was he always naked except for that leather belt around the waist or had the game makers taken his clothes? It seemed the wrong moment to ask.

His eyes lit up when he peeked inside. "We'll be eating well tonight! This one is full of ration packs. They're old, very old, but they're the fancy ones that basically last forever and don't taste like sawdust. We can have some together with the food the chii gave us and take more with us for when we move on."

He pulled a couple of small squares wrapped in yellow foil from the crate. Something was off about his movements. They were jerky, as if he didn't have full control over his muscles.

"Is everything alright?" I asked before I could stop myself.

He didn't look at me when he replied. "I'm not good with cold. This cave is cooler than I expected."

Of course! He was a snake. Well, half a snake. It shouldn't surprise me that he was cold-blooded and needed warmth to function.

I dropped the bundle of blankets I'd been carrying and undid the rope the chii had tied around them. There were four of them, all thin and light, but the chii had promised that they would be warmer than they looked.

"We cannot rest yet," Venom said, but his gaze longingly lingered on the blankets. "We should investigate this cave a little further, so we know for sure that we're safe here."

One of the yellow food packs slipped from his fingers as if to contradict his words.

I held out one of the blankets. "Wrap yourself into this and we'll find a comfy place to camp. I think I'd like to stay close to where we came in, just in case."

I scanned the crates scattered beneath the cave entrance. One, almost reaching the top of the ledge, was on its side, creating a sort of cave within a cave. With the way it was turned, it might shelter us from the cool draught that was licking at my skin, tempting me to take one of the blankets for myself.

"Over there." I led Venom to the crate. He followed slowly, his movements no longer smooth and elegant.

He was clearly struggling. Somehow, he managed to hold on to the remaining food parcels.

I spread one of the blankets over the metal floor, then pointed at it. "Sit."

He raised a scaled brow. "Are you giving me orders?"

"Yes."

Venom smirked. "Who am I to refuse. Females are always right, my mother used to say."

As soon as he had curled up his tail around his body, making himself less of a target for the cold, I wrapped another blanket around him. My hands touched his scales, and I paused for just a moment. They were cool yet still held a lingering warmth that seeped into my skin. The scales were softer than I'd thought. Those sharp rocks outside must have been very uncomfortable for Venom.

I quickly pulled back and pretended that this hadn't happened. It was entirely inappropriate to be touching him. I should keep my distance and hope he'd forget about all the strange things he'd mentioned at our first encounter. I really preferred the head-in-the-sand method for the topic of mates and relationships and destiny.

I wrapped a blanket around my shoulders like a cloak. There was less of a draught in this crate, but it was still chilly.

Venom had crossed his arms in front of his chest, pulling his blankets tightly around his body. Poor guy. I wished I could have started a fire, but there was neither wood nor matches. Maybe some of the crates held useful items, but how long would it take to go through all of them? We'd been lucky that the one holding the food pouches had been left unlocked.

"Tell me how to make this food," I said, taking a seat opposite Venom. The blanket was surprisingly soft, even though it looked like it was made of grass. I wasn't sure what kind of plant it had been woven from, but whatever it was, it protected us effectively from the cold metal floor.

Venom shot me strange look. "You shall not cook for me, mate. That is my job. I am to provide for you. Now and always."

"Go easy on the mate talk," I warned. "You said we'd discuss that after we've somehow escaped this planet."

"Apologies. But the point stands. I will not let you demean yourself by offering me food. That is the male's task."

"On my planet, both men and women do the cooking. In the past, it was mostly the women, but nowadays, men have learned they are just as capable of handling a wooden spoon as their wives and mothers are."

"What do they do with that wooden spoon?" Venom asked, sounding genuinely confused. I was about to answer when he grinned. "I am just teasing. Although I'm sure spoons have many uses."

Was that an innuendo? Or was I interpreting something into an innocent comment?

To distract myself, I handed him one of the food pouches that had fallen to the ground. "How do you do this?"

Venom grimaced. "With great difficulty."

15

VENOM

Moving was fucking hard. My muscles were locked into place, my energy quickly leaving me. My body was desperate to shut down until warmth returned. But I couldn't. Not while I had my mate with me. I had to guard her. Look after her. Provide her with food.

What a silly idea she had, cooking for me. Did she not know that females were not supposed to trouble themselves with such mundane, menial tasks? We'd have to learn much about our different cultures. And while I was open to trying some of her traditions, I would not budge on this tonight. I was going to make my first meal for her. And if she let me, I would give her the first dose of my venom. I wasn't looking forward to that conversation, but it needed to be discussed. She had to know what nagas were capable of.

But first, I had to persuade my muscles to move. I reached out for the pouch, every cell screaming in protest. Fuck. I gripped it with shaking, clumsy fingers, praying to all the gods that I wouldn't drop it and embarrass myself. There was no way of hiding my weakness. It was too cold.

"You open it by pulling this tab," I explained. My tongue was sluggish. Soon, I'd be unable to talk. But if I was lucky, this ration hadn't lost its instaheat properties yet. "Then you twist the seal at the bottom which starts a chemical reaction inside. See the steam? Make sure not to get your hands above a pouch while it's processing or you'll burn yourself. The food will be ready in a click or two. You'll find utensils attached to the side, under that label."

I sat the ration down in front of my mate and opened a second one for myself. Disregarding my own advice, I held my right hand above the pouch. My scales could handle the heat. Warmth seeped through my scales, travelling up my arm. I wriggled my fingers, suddenly more flexible again. It wouldn't last long, but I would enjoy it while I could.

"What kind of food is this?" my mate asked. "It smells kind of fishy."

"I cannot fully read the label, it is not written in Intergalactic Standard. Maybe it is a dialect the early game makers spoke. If I'm not mistaken, this word means 'avian'. But I could be entirely wrong. Does it matter?"

She gave the pouch a sniff. "I suppose not. It's edible for me, right? It won't poison me?"

No, but I might.

I cleared my throat. "No, it won't. But before we

eat, I have to ask your permission to..." I sighed. She was going to get scared. But this could save her life. I had to.

I slowly extended my fangs to their full length, watching her closely. "Nagas are venomous. The venom contained in my fangs can kill."

She did not look scared, only curious. "Could you kill the monster that chased me?"

"A prondu? Unlikely. But my venom would hurt, maybe even paralyse. It would be enough to give me the time to get away. That's more important than killing the beast. It is not evil by nature. Only hungry."

Clare grimaced. "It looked very hungry."

"The game makers would have made sure that it was. It looks better on camera if the monsters are crazed with hunger, taking risks they wouldn't otherwise. But going back to my fangs. The venom in them might not be enough to kill a prondu, but it would be lethal to you. Not that I would ever hurt you. Never."

"Then what is the problem?"

"I know I said I would not talk about it again, but it is important. A naga's venom has healing properties for one person only: their mate. We don't know what we will face out there tomorrow, or in the days to come. I want to be able to help you should you get injured."

She cocked her head to the side, her gaze fixed on my fangs. "Do you want my permission to bite me in an emergency?"

"Yes, but that is not all. If I bit you now, it would kill you. Your body needs to get used to my venom first.

It will be enough for me to add two drops to your food. You might feel a little queasy afterwards, but having a full stomach should help. And I... I will need to drink your blood."

Now she looked a little scared. "Please don't tell me you're a vampire?"

"What's that?"

"Bloodsuckers that can turn into bats. Well, it depends on which story you read. Dracula is very different from Edward. Anyway. Are you a vampire?"

"I can assure you that I am a not. All I need is a drop of your blood so that my body can change the venom's toxicity into something that is no longer lethal to you. I suppose it's like I'm teaching my venom that you are my mate and that you are not to be harmed."

"Only one drop?" She seemed relieved.

"I promise. I will prick your finger and you shall hold it over my mouth. I cannot mix your blood with my food like we will do with my venom. It has to be fresh."

"You are a vampire," she muttered, but it was light-hearted, not with fear. "Are there any other side effects I should know about?"

"Nobody has ever done this with a Peritan," I admitted. "But we are mates, Glycon be praised. We are destined to be together. You will not-"

She held a finger to her lips. I stopped talking, even though I wasn't sure what she was doing. Was she about to bite her finger to provide me with her blood?

I pulled the axe from beneath my blankets. "Do not bite yourself. We shall use the axe."

Clare gave it a doubtful look. "I wasn't about to bite my finger. That gesture was meant for you to shut up. You were talking mates again. You really have to stop doing that."

I wanted to argue. Tell her that we were mates. That this was real. She had to feel it. Surely, she felt it in her heart, in her soul. We were meant to be together. Now and forever. It didn't matter that we were different species, coming together in the deadliest place in the galaxy. None of it mattered. She was my mate.

"If we're using the axe, then I'm going to do it myself," she said. Before I could stop her, she'd pressed her left thumb to the blade, nicking her skin. I could smell her blood immediately. It was sweet, so very sweet, like ripe fruit on a summer's day.

I made myself smaller and bent my head back, exposing my throat. If she'd been a naga, she knew that I would only show such vulnerability in the presence of my mate or my parents. I opened my mouth, my fangs still extended, and waited for the drop of her lifeblood.

I felt a little self-conscious. Until now, I had tried to keep my forked tongue out of sight. There were many species across the universe who saw it as a symbol of evil – not that I'd ever understood why. But nagas were generally misunderstood, so it shouldn't have surprised me. We were seen as tricksters, criminals, the worst of the worst. I was glad that my mate had grown up on a backwater planet where she wouldn't have been exposed to such rumours.

The moment the drop of blood hit my tongue, bolts of electricity raced all across my body, down to the very tip of my tail. I gasped for air, taken aback by the severity of the reaction, before I managed to pull back control. I closed my eyes for a moment to enjoy the feeling of bliss now spreading through me. The blood tasted of iron and commitment, a promise of bonds too strong to break. I swallowed it, savouring the taste, then looked at my mate with a smile.

"Thank you. It means more than I can put into words."

She pointed at her ration pouch. "I guess it's time for you to add your venom now?"

I pictured a prondu, rearing up and about to attack. My venom glands shot into action, pushing the liquid down into my fangs. I expressed two small drops, letting them fall into her food. This was not the traditional way of doing it, without witnesses or official ceremony, but it would have to do.

She stared at the pouch with an expression I interpreted as curiosity, but it could have been distaste. Peritans were clearly a species not used to drinking each other's blood. Not that nagas did that regularly. We had a reputation for all sorts of nasty behaviours, but sucking blood was not one of them. What had she called it? Vampire?

"To your health," she said and raised the pouch to her lips. I watched tensely, my breath stuck in my throat, as she swallowed the first mouthful. There was no way for me to tell if the blood had done its job. Please, Glycon, let this work.

Clare grimaced. "Not the best meal I've ever had, but also not the worst. What is this stuff?"

"A carefully chosen mix of nutrients that offers optimal sustenance to a wide range of species. At least that's what they usually contain. It's not real food, it's made in a lab. But it will keep us going for a while."

"Are you not going to eat yours?" she asked, nodding at the pouch I was still holding. Most of the heat had dissipated, but the food would hopefully still be lukewarm.

I could think of better things to eat – the lush taste of her blood still swirled in my mouth – but I needed the warmth. I could already feel the muscles in my tail lock up again. The blankets weren't enough to keep me at the temperature I needed to function. The ration packs would keep me going for a bit, but not all night.

If the game makers attacked us during the night, I would be defenceless. The thought of not being able to fight for my mate chilled me more than the cool air.

16

CLARE

When we'd both finished our meal, I was full, warm and in surprisingly good spirits. Yes, we were on a hostile alien planet, but I'd enjoyed getting to know Venom a little more. I'd got used to seeing his sharp fangs when he smiled and had come to appreciate his sense of humour. We may have been from different species but that didn't mean we couldn't laugh about the same things.

"What's for dessert?" I joked.

"If you're still hungry, I can prepare another ration for you. Or you could snack on the berries the chii gave us."

I rubbed my belly. "I'm not sure I could eat even a single berry. This was so filling."

"It is supposed to be. And you just ate a portion created for a species much b-bigger than you."

He shivered slightly. Was he getting cold again

already? I was slightly chilly now that I'd stopped eating, but the meal had warmed me from the inside.

"I can look for more blankets," I offered.

He gave a small shake of his head, his long black hair sliding over one shoulder. "I highly doubt we'll find any here. The game makers wouldn't send items of comfort down here. Food, yes, b-but the rest will be weapons, technology, tools to keep the resident monsters in check. There won't be any blankets. We're lucky the chii thought ahead and g-gave us ours."

His words came out stiffly, lips tight, fangs barely visible. He was trying to control the tremble in his voice, but I could hear it anyway. He wasn't just chilly – he was freezing.

"That's not good enough," I said, rising to my knees. "You're no use to either of us if you turn into a naga popsicle."

"I will b-be fine."

I raised an eyebrow at his chattering voice. "Are you sure about that? I don't know much about your species, but if you're even slightly similar to the reptiles we have on Earth, you need warmth to function."

"I will be fine," he repeated. He refused to look at me, which told me everything I needed to know.

I narrowed my eyes. "Liar."

He huffed a breath that might have been a laugh. "I'm trying to b-be optimistic."

"Optimism doesn't keep you warm." I shuffled closer and reached for the blanket I had wrapped around my shoulders. "We'll share this one. If we sit beneath a blanket together, my body heat should warm you as well. Do you think that will help?"

He didn't move. "Clare..."

"What?"

"This might... n-not b-be safe."

I paused. "Are you going to hurt me?"

"N-never." His voice cracked like ice.

I held his gaze, steady despite the shiver down my spine that had nothing to do with the cold.

He wasn't trying to scare me – if anything, he looked scared of himself.

"I trust you," I said quietly. I wasn't sure why I said that – I didn't know him, knew barely anything about him, and yet... It was true. I trusted him. And my instincts were always right. Maybe it was the chii. I trusted them and they trusted Venom. They had formed a bond with both of us. That had to count for something.

His eyes widened. "You shouldn't. If I g-get too close to you so soon after tasting your b-blood... I don't know if I'll be able t-to stop myself."

I hesitated, my fingers tightening around the blanket. That wasn't what I'd expected him to say. I'd thought he was worried about impropriety or physical awkwardness – not losing control because he'd tasted me.

"You mean like some kind of predator instinct?" I asked carefully.

His throat bobbed as he swallowed. "Yes. N-no. It's m-more complicated than that."

"That's not very reassuring."

He finally met my gaze, and the look in his eyes made my breath catch. It wasn't hunger, not exactly. It was fear. Of himself.

"I've t-trained for years to k-keep it contained," he said softly. "B-but training can only g-go so f-far. Especially when the scent is... overwhelming."

I didn't know what to say to that. My brain skittered between questions. Did I want to know what I smelled like to him? Was this just about the blood? Or something more primal, more...dangerous?

"And what if I tell you I'm not scared?" I said, but the words came out softer than I meant them to.

He didn't smile. "Then I'd say you d-don't know enough about me yet."

A beat of silence passed. The air between us was thick with tension – not quite sexual, not quite hostile. Just wary. Charged.

I took a deep breath. "Okay. Then tell me."

He blinked. "What?"

"Tell me what I don't know. Help me understand what you are... what this is. Because if we're stuck together, and sharing a blanket is going to turn you into a slavering beast, I think I deserve to be informed in advance."

That got a reaction – a soft snort, almost a laugh. His fangs flashed. The tension in his shoulders eased a fraction.

"I'm not g-going t-to attack you," he said. "But m-my instincts... they're n-not subtle. When I'm near you, especially after b-blood has been exchanged, they want things I m-might not."

I frowned. "Like what?"

He hesitated. "To m-mate."

Oh. Fuck. We were back to the mating talk. Although I was pretty sure that this time, he didn't mean being in a relationship. He was talking about sex.

I swallowed. "And do *you* want that?"

Another silence. Then, with agonising restraint: "Yes. B-but not like this."

I found myself relaxing, just a little. That mattered. It meant he was still in control, even if something more primal was tugging at him beneath the surface.

I unwrapped the blanket from my shoulders and held it open between us. Cool air kissed my skin despite the scarves I had wrapped all around my body. The blanket had kept the chill out more than I'd realised.

"Then we do this carefully," I said. "For warmth. Nothing else. If you feel like you can't hold back, tell me. Communicate. I will move away if it becomes too difficult for you."

He studied me, long and hard. "Y-you're sure?"

"Yes."

I moved first. Quietly, deliberately, I crossed the space between us and sat down beside him. Close, but not quite touching. I draped the blanket around our shoulders like a tent, leaving a gap between our bodies, though I could feel the cold radiate from his scales. He was even more hypothermic than I'd feared.

He didn't move. Didn't reach for me. Just sat perfectly still, his tail coiled neatly around him, hands folded in his lap like he was meditating on a knife's edge.

Neither of us spoke.

The silence between us wasn't uncomfortable, exactly. Just tight. Charged. Like the air before a storm.

But he didn't touch me. Didn't push.

And I didn't lean in.

We sat there, shoulder to not-quite-shoulder, two beings wrapped in the same blanket, pretending it was just about the cold. Which it was, right?

I kept my arms tucked in, hands in my lap, determined not to touch him.

And yet...

I could feel him beside me, every still inch of him. The coolness of his skin radiated even through the shared cover. I could smell him too – not in a bad way. Not even in an alien way. Just... Venom. Clean, metallic, with a faint tang of something earthy and sharp like crushed herbs. It curled into my nose with every breath and settled low in my belly like a satisfying heaviness. I liked his smell.

Which made no sense. He wasn't human. He wasn't even humanoid.

But that didn't stop the way my skin prickled with awareness.

I didn't know him.

He was dangerous.

He was trying not to be.

And I... was losing the battle to keep my guard up.

I pressed my lips together, glancing sideways at him.

He was pale – not in colour exactly, but in energy. His eyes were half-closed, his shoulders slightly hunched. A tremor passed through his muscles, barely visible but constant.

"Venom?" I asked quietly.

He didn't respond.

My stomach twisted. "Venom!" I reached out and touched his arm. He flinched, but the movement was jerky and uncontrolled.

"S-still... f-fine," he muttered, his teeth chattering audibly.

Liar.

His slitted eyes had drifted half-closed, and a visible shiver rippled through his upper body. He wasn't just cold. He was on the verge of shutting down.

A bolt of concern shot through me. I didn't understand everything about his biology, but this was bad. He was trying so hard to hold himself together, to fight his instincts, to give me space. But if he kept going like this, he might not make it through the night.

I didn't think. I just acted. I slipped an arm around his waist and shuffled closer until our sides touched fully beneath the blanket. My bare skin met the chill of his scales, and I bit back a gasp. He was freezing. Absolutely freezing. A living, breathing being shouldn't feel this cold. Goosebumps ran over my skin.

"I'm not doing this for you," I muttered, more to

myself than to him. "You're just no good to me half-frozen."

He didn't resist. Didn't speak. He just let out a slow exhale and leaned slightly into me, like the last thread of tension had snapped.

I pulled him closer, wrapping myself around him as much as I could by hugging him like a koala, one leg on either side of him. He was so much bigger than me, so I had to make it count.

"Don't look under the blanket," I muttered, and pulled some of the carefully wrapped scarves off my body. My arms and legs were first, but it wouldn't be enough. I left only one scarf wrapped around my boobs and one slung around my waist. For modesty. But if this wasn't enough, I knew I was prepared to take it all off. His life was more important than my sense of modesty.

His scales were almost as soft as human skin. I'd expected to feel the overlaps between them, but no. They were cold, so very cold. I felt more and more helpless. My body heat wasn't going to be enough to warm this huge alien.

His arm came up automatically, loosely circling my back. The rest of him – his long, coiled tail – shifted with a faint rustle as it curled nearer, cocooning us in gentle loops. Not tight, not possessive. Just *there*. Protective.

My heart was racing now, but not from fear.

I didn't know what this was. Didn't understand why I wanted to press closer, or why his scent made something in my chest ache. I barely knew him.

But I knew he made me feel safe. And seen.

I could feel the restraint in him, the careful way he had placed his coils, the way his hand barely touched my back. His breathing was shallow.

And fuck, he was cold. My skin prickled from the chill radiating off his torso, and yet something in me wanted to stay there. To melt into him.

I told myself it was just adrenaline. A survival reaction. Proximity in extreme conditions. But it wasn't just that. Not really.

I was attracted to him. I didn't know why – maybe it was the way he spoke to me like an equal, the dry humour, the rare flickers of vulnerability that slipped through his fanged façade. Maybe it was the way he looked at me, like I was more than a prize in a game.

Whatever it was, it was growing harder to ignore.

"You're still shaking," I said softly.

"I'll b-be alright," he replied, though it sounded more like an automatic defence than truth.

I hugged him tighter. His hip pushed against my core.

He inhaled sharply.

"I'm not going to break," I said. "And I don't scare easily."

His eyes flicked to mine, glowing faintly in the dark. "I'm n-not afraid of you, Clare. I'm af-fraid *for* you."

My heart skipped a beat.

Without thinking, I reached up and touched his face – just a light brush of my fingertips along his cheekbone, where larger plates gave way to scales so tiny they almost resembled skin.

"Then stop freezing and take the warmth I'm offering."

His hand rose slowly, almost reverently, and settled on my waist. Not pulling. Just resting.

We stayed like that for a breathless moment.

Then another.

And when he turned his face towards mine, his lips parted slightly, eyes dark with something that wasn't hunger – not exactly – but need, I stopped thinking altogether.

I leaned in and kissed him.

17

VENOM

She kissed me.

Not the cautious brush of someone testing a theory. Not the desperate attempt of someone alone and scared searching for comfort.

A real kiss. Soft and deliberate. Trusting.

I should have pulled away. I knew I should.

Instead, I froze.

Not from the cold this time – though I could still feel it clinging to my limbs like chains, slow and creeping, stopping me from functioning. From the shock of her lips on mine. From the heat of her skin. From the roaring, rising wave inside me that had nothing to do with logic and everything to do with *her*.

Clare.

My mate.

The one I had promised restraint. The one I wasn't supposed to touch, not until we were safe.

I kissed her back.

Just once. Just enough to taste the breath between us, to feel the shiver that ran through her when I opened my mouth and touched hers fully. I was careful to keep my fangs pulled back, leaving just the tips exposed. As much as I craved to bite her, claim her as mine, I knew that she was not ready.

And then I tore myself away, breath ragged, the ache in my chest almost worse than the cold.

"This is a mistake," I rasped. My teeth were no longer chattering.

She didn't flinch. She just looked at me like I'd said the sky was purple. "Why?"

I closed my eyes. "Because I want more."

She was silent for a moment. I could feel her still pressed against me, all soft skin and steady warmth and alluring scent.

"Then say stop," she said quietly. "And I will. Right now."

I opened my eyes and looked at her. Really looked.

She wasn't seducing me. Wasn't playing some kind of game. She was offering – on her terms. And giving me the choice.

No one had ever done that before.

"I don't want to stop," I admitted. The words came out raw. "But I don't want to lose control either."

"You won't," she said.

Glycon help me, I believed her.

Her body shifted against mine, her thighs hugging

my waist, her arms warm and steady around me. My coils had already begun to encircle her without conscious thought.

I forced myself to still them.

She noticed. Of course she did. She was observant like that.

"It's alright," she said softly. "You're cold. You need this."

I needed so much more than warmth.

I needed *her*.

But more than that – I needed control.

Because I could feel the shift starting. Deep in my core. That low, coiled pull of instinct unravelling. My body preparing for what it believed was inevitable.

One of my cocks began to stir – a pressure low in my abdomen, subtle but insistent, pushing against the sheath that kept it protected and hidden. That part of me I could summon at will. The functional part. The part used for pleasure, bonding, sex that didn't matter.

But the other...

The other was waiting.

That was the one I feared. The one that would only emerge for *her*. Once she was ready.

Clare kissed me again.

Slow, tender, exploratory. Her lips moved against mine with no urgency, no pressure. Just shared heat, and care, and that maddening scent that had sunk into my blood like a drug.

I wanted more of her. Everything. And I would give my all to her.

I could feel her legs still wrapped around my waist, the press of her breasts against my chest. Her skin was fever-warm against mine.

I was no longer as cold as I had been. It wasn't just her body warmth that was doing the trick. It was the heat between us, intangible and yet more effective than anything a thermometer could track.

My tail twitched. Without thought, the tip slipped from the blanket and brushed the edge of her thigh. She shivered – not in fear, but in reaction. Encouragement.

Carefully, slowly, I brought the tip up, circling behind her back and curving along her spine. She arched slightly. My tail slid higher, teasing the edge of the scarf she'd left wrapped around her chest.

"Is this alright?" I murmured.

She nodded. Breathless. "More than."

I let the tip of my tail flick gently over one breast, the fabric of the scarf slipping with each pass. Her breath hitched, and her hips shifted against me.

I groaned. "Clare..."

She looked up at me, eyes dark and steady. "Yes?"

"I'm close to a line I can't uncross."

Her hands slid down to rest on my hips, just above where the blanket pooled. "Then tell me what that line is."

I exhaled shakily. "You know I'm not built like you."

"I gathered." She smiled – teasing, warm. "Explain it to me."

I swallowed. This was not a conversation I ever expected to have like this, especially not while every instinct in me was sharpening to a point.

"I have... two," I said at last. "Cocks. Usually inverted. They only emerge when needed."

Her brow rose, but she said nothing. She was listening.

"I can control one," I continued. "It's... compatible. It responds to arousal, readiness, choice."

"And the other?"

I hesitated.

"The other only comes out for a fated mate. I can't summon it. I can't *not* summon it. If it starts... I'll know."

"And so will I?" she asked.

I nodded.

Her lips parted slightly. "And is it... starting?"

I looked down at her, at the way she was pressed against me, breathing fast but not afraid.

"Yes, but I can still control it," I said hoarsely. "But what is getting harder to control is the urge to bite you."

Her breath caught.

I felt her heartbeat against my chest. Strong. Not panicked. Excited.

"Would it hurt?" she asked, voice barely above a whisper.

I closed my eyes. "Not in the way you think. But it would mark you. Permanently. I don't want to take that from you without knowing you want it."

She was silent for a long moment. Then she leaned forward, her forehead resting against mine.

"The chii have already marked me. They didn't ask for permission. I appreciate you did. And you're right. I don't know if I want that. But I also don't want you to stop touching me either."

"Touching?" I asked hoarsely.

"Maybe more." Her gaze flicked down my body, as if searching for my cocks.

My restraint snapped – not into violence, not into frenzy. But into action.

I shifted, laying her gently down on the folded coils of my tail, cushioning her from the cold metal floor. She gasped as I wrapped her in my body – not trapping, just holding. Secure.

The blankets pooled around us like a cocoon.

My hand slid along her side, down to her thigh. She shifted, opening herself to me, her body inviting, warm, human – and mine.

And slowly, reverently, I let myself respond.

One cock extended, sliding free from the protective slit at my groin. Just one. The one I could choose.

The other stayed hidden.

And for now... that was enough.

Clare was beneath me, nestled in the cradle of my coils, eyes wide and dark and full of need.

She'd told me not to stop.

So I didn't.

My fangs extended. It was no longer under my control.

I shifted above her, adjusting so that my cock – thick, ridged, flushed dark with arousal – pressed gently against the seam of her thighs. I was careful, slow, giving her every chance to pull away.

She didn't.

Her hips bucked up instinctively, seeking my cock. I groaned low in my throat, the sound vibrating between us as I rocked against her, once, twice, the motion slow and teasing. Her thighs tensed around me, and her breath came faster.

I used the tip of my tail to stroke over one breast again, the scarf slipping aside under the gentle pressure. Her nipple hardened, and I circled it lazily, drawing a breathy moan from her lips.

"Is this alright?" I asked.

"Don't you dare stop," she whispered hoarsely.

That was all the permission I needed.

I hooked one arm under her thigh and drew her closer. My cock slid through the slick heat between her legs, unhurried, savouring every inch of contact. She was soaked – warm, welcoming, her body ready for mine.

I angled myself, pressing the head of my cock against her entrance. She shifted beneath me, bracing one hand on my chest, the other gripping my wrist where I held her.

"Wait," she said softly.

I stilled immediately. "Too much?"

She shook her head. "No. Just... let me look at you for a second."

I did. Let her take in the reality of what we were doing. She looked between us, and I followed her gaze. Our bodies were bathed in shadow beneath the blanket, but I was sure she was able to make out my cock, hard and eager.

"So big," she muttered. "And...different."

"I won't hurt you. I'll go slow," I promised.

Her fingers flexed, and then she nodded.

"Okay. Now."

I pushed forward.

She gasped, her mouth parting in a silent cry as I stretched her slowly, inch by inch. I moved carefully, giving her time, watching her face for every flicker of tension or hesitation.

"Clare..."

"I'm fine," she breathed, voice trembling. "Keep going."

I slid deeper, the ridges along my cock dragging against her inner walls in a way that made her moan aloud. Her back arched, her hips lifting to meet mine. She took all of me, inch by thick inch, until I was buried to the base.

Fuck, she was tight.

And perfect.

I stayed still for a moment, letting her adjust, my forehead pressed to hers, her breath mingling with mine. Her body trembled around me, not from fear or discomfort – but from the sheer intensity of it.

When she finally rolled her hips, I groaned and began to move.

Slow strokes at first, savouring her, every thrust a delicious slide of heat and friction. Her fingers dug into my arms. Her moans grew louder, breathier. I angled my hips, changing the depth until I found the spot that made her cry out, her body clenching around me.

"There," she gasped. "Oh gods, there–"

I gave her everything. Every ounce of control, of restraint, of instinct honed over years of discipline – all undone, all poured into the rhythm of my body moving against hers.

My other cock was fighting against its protective sheath, against the control I wielded over it. I held on by a scale's width. I couldn't go back on my promise to her. I couldn't go further than this tonight.

My tail tightened around her delicate body, not trapping, just holding her still as I fucked her, each thrust driving deeper, stronger, her cries growing wild.

She shattered around me with a choked cry, her back bowing, her legs shaking. The way she clenched down on me sent me spiralling.

I growled, low and feral, as I came, buried deep inside her, my cock pulsing as I spilled everything into her warmth.

I didn't bite her.

I wanted to. Every nerve screamed for it. But I didn't.

Instead, I held her. Let the tension drain from my body as she curled against me.

My tail loosened. My arms stayed wrapped around her.

Her hand drifted up to my chest, her cheek resting above my hearts.

"Still cold?" she asked, voice barely a whisper.

I kissed the crown of her head. "Never again."

18

CLARE

I woke with a start. I'd had a dream, something about curling around a tree like a snake while feeling the sun's soothing rays on my scales, before the forest had erupted into fire. For a moment, I didn't know where I was. Then I felt the scales against my cheek, the heavy tail wrapped around my legs, and I remembered.

Venom.

I had slept with Venom.

Fuck.

I didn't move. I wasn't sure I *could* move. His coils were heavy across my legs, not crushing but anchoring. His chest rose and fell steadily beneath my cheek, and the cave was still wrapped in that same hushed stillness as the night before.

I'd slept with him.

Not just shared heat. Not just survival huddling. I'd *wanted* it. Asked for it. Enjoyed it.

And now I was lying here, tangled up in a naga's

embrace, half-naked, on a hostile alien planet, wondering what the hell was wrong with me.

My stomach twisted with regret, but I didn't quite know what I was regretting. Not the sex itself – that had been... gods, it had been *good*. Not just the physical part, either. The way he touched me, the way he'd held back. The way he'd *looked* at me.

His cock had been alien and yet perfect for me, like a key created to fit into my lock. It had been too dark to make out all the details, but there had been bulging rings around the shaft that had most definitely contributed to the best orgasm I'd ever experienced.

But still, the shame and regret didn't disappear at the memory of how I'd come apart. Had it been too soon? Too reckless? Too much?

We'd met that day. Some time in the afternoon.

And I'd been ready to climb him like a tree by nightfall.

I closed my eyes and breathed through the knot in my chest. Who was going to judge me? My friends? My family? They were further away than I could even imagine.

No. This wasn't about them. It was about *Earth*. About old rules and expectations that no longer applied to the person I was becoming.

Earth was far away. So were the people who'd raised me to believe love had a formula, that desire needed a waiting period, that you had to earn intimacy with time and social approval.

There was no approval to be found here. No society. No rules.

Just me. And Venom. And the wild beating of my own heart.

I shifted slightly, and his arm tightened instinctively around my waist. Not possessive. Just... responsive.

My guilt didn't vanish, but it softened. I didn't need to justify my choices to a world I no longer lived in.

I was allowed to want something – someone – for no other reason than that it felt right.

Especially in a place like this. Where every moment might be our last.

The air shifted. A faint clicking sound echoed near the cave entrance.

Venom stirred beneath me. His eyes opened – slitted, glowing faintly green in the dim light. "Clare?" he murmured.

"I'm awake."

He tensed, not at my words but at something else. A vibration under the stone. A sound beyond what I could hear.

"Something's wrong," I said.

At the same time, Sa'quii's voice rang in my head. From Venom's expression I could tell that he was hearing the chii as well.

More drones have joined the first. They are watching all exits to the cave. Other chii have arrived with news. Big Ones are gathering in the valley below. And monsters. So many monsters.

She sounded worried.

Venom sat up at once, coils shifting beneath me. "How many drones?"

Six. Two look different than the rest.

She sent us a mental image. It didn't mean anything to me, but Venom sucked in a sharp breath.

"Those are weaponised drones. They can injure or even kill. If I'm not mistaken, they'll also have tranquiliser darts on board. The game makers sometimes use those on contestants if they're in an area low on monsters. They then move the unconscious contestant to a place more suited for drama."

I didn't like the sound of that. "Drama?" I asked.

"Violent death by monster." Venom's jaw clenched. "They're forcing movement. Trying to flush us."

I pulled the blanket tighter around my body, the chill of the cave suddenly far more noticeable. "Can we contact the Bloodstar? Or someone else?"

"I'd need a terminal, a computer to contact them. There are many layers of security wrapped around this planet, so to speak, and I don't have access to the technology I'd need to hack them. I have called for help from the IA, but I don't know if and when and even how they'll reply."

We have found many tools the Big Ones left behind, Sa'quii chimed in. *Maybe you will find what you need in the cave. I can send some of my people through the hidden paths. They will not be spotted by the drones.*

"We shall start searching," Venom said. He was already scanning the cave walls, his coils loosening around me. I climbed off him, searching for the scarves I'd discarded last night to give me some more cover.

"Are you not too cold?" I asked Venom as a cool breeze made my gooseflesh rise.

"A little, but movement will help. The sun has risen and the cave is getting warmer already. However, I need to thank you for what you did for me last night. Without you... I would not be in the condition I am now. Thank you, from the bottom of my hearts."

"Hearts?" I repeated weakly.

He grinned. "Two of them."

"Two hearts, two cocks. Anything else you have two of?"

He flashed his fangs at me in reply, then rose to his full height in a smooth motion. He looked fully recovered, which reassured me massively. I'd really been worried last night.

While I got dressed – if you could call it that – he left the crate to examine the cave further. I packed up the blankets, stashing the remaining food rations in Venom's bag. I wanted to be ready to leave if we had to make a quick exit.

"Clare?" Venom called from just outside the crate. "There might be a relay node buried in the bedrock. I think this was once a control chamber, before it was turned into storage. We'll need to find old wiring. Something intact."

"I'll help," I said, wrapping the scarf more tightly around my shoulders before stepping out of the crate.

The cavern stretched around us like the ribcage of

some colossal beast, the black stone ceiling arched high above and glittering faintly where patches of diamond caught the filtered sunlight. The glowing orbs along the walls gave off a cold, bluish sheen that deepened every shadow.

Crates towered over us – some the size of kitchen cupboards, others large enough to house entire vehicles. I half expected one of them to start beeping or unfolding into a killer drone. Nothing moved. Yet.

Venom slithered toward the far side, his coils silent on the stone. "The fact that these orbs still work means there is electricity routed through the stone. I assume they run on solar power, fully automated, but there still needs to be a control panel to adjust the lights. Help me look for embedded panels or wiring – anything out of place. Focus near the back wall. Control tech would have been placed away from obvious access points."

We split up. I would have preferred to stay with him. This cave was giving me the creeps, especially knowing that we were surrounded by drones on the outside. But it made sense to cover two directions at once.

I skirted around the larger crates, brushing my fingers across the stone behind them. Nothing but cold rock at first. Then I found a section where the wall felt... wrong. Warmer. Smoother. As if it had been polished, once.

"Here," I called, waving Venom over.

He reached me in seconds, inspecting the spot with

narrowed eyes. "It's not a seam, but it's newer than the rest. Stand back."

He grabbed a thin metal rod from a pile of discarded tools on the ground and scraped it along the smooth section. We waited.

Nothing.

Then he opened his palm and held it to my mouth.

"Breathe on it."

I shot him a questioning look but then exhaled a slow breath. He pressed that hand to the wall, wriggling his fingers slightly.

Click.

A section of the black rock slid back with a hiss of pressure. Dust drifted down. Inside: wires, old data ports, and a glowing interface screen barely brighter than an ember. The symbols on the screen meant nothing to me, but Venom exhaled sharply. "By the stars... it's still live."

I peered over his shoulder. "What now?"

"Now I patch in, break through any security they might have, strip the data load, and try to route a burst transmission through one of the ancient orbital relays. Nobody ever bothered to remove them. I've been telling the game makers for ages that they pose a security risk, but nobody listened to me. Now we can make good use of them. If the Bloodstar is still watching this region, they might catch it."

"And if the game makers intercept it first?"

"Then they'll come straight here. Harder. Faster. No more waiting outside the cave to flush us out. They will sacrifice the crowd's entertainment to get their revenge on me."

I swallowed. "No pressure then."

He met my gaze. "We'll send one signal. No fancy encryption, just coordinates and a distress call."

"Just tell me where to run if this goes to hell."

"You'll be running with me."

19

VENOM

The moment I pressed the final command, the interface went dark.

No confirmation. No echo. Just the faint hum of buried circuitry and the low pulse of power fading into the stone.

I waited. One breath. Then another.

Nothing.

"Did it work?" Clare asked behind me.

"I don't know," I admitted. "If they received it, they'll come. If not…"

I didn't finish the sentence.

Before the silence could stretch further, a familiar chirping sound echoed from the tunnel. I turned just as a cluster of chii emerged, running on all fours, their tails erect. At the front was Ba'quoo, standing out with his silver feathers among his golden and bronze companions.

He scrambled up a crate and fixed me with all three eyes. His presence pressed against my mind a moment before his voice did.

More movement. Many beasts. Bigger than any we have seen here before. Wings. Fire. The sky trembles.

"Can you show me?" I asked sharply.

I have not seen them myself. But this is what Cla'quoo witnessed.

The image he sent was blurry around the edges and somewhat faded, but it was clear enough for me to recognise the monster.

"Fuck," I exclaimed before I could stop myself. "That's Tyvaron!"

"What's that?" Clare asked, her voice tight. "It looks to me like a dragon. I mean, an alien dragon, but somewhat similar."

I nodded once, eyes fixed on the hazy image still flickering in my mind. "I have read about dragons from Peritan mythology. The Tyvarin were engineered during the Skarn Rebellions on a planet far away from here – biomechanical sky-beasts, grown in labs and hardwired with tactical systems. They weren't just weapons. They could think. Learn. Adapt. Cyborgs with wings and the ability to breathe fire."

I drew in a breath. "The one Ba'quoo showed us isn't just any Tyvarin. That's Tyvaron."

"Like... a name?"

"A designation. The first and only of its class. A prototype designed for high-altitude domination and autonomous combat decisions. Its creators gave it partial sentience. Enough to assess threats, react, even disobey if survival logic dictated."

Her brows furrowed. "You're telling me that thing's smart?"

I nodded grimly. "It was supposed to be a commander-beast. The project was shut down when it turned on its own handlers during testing. They tried to wipe its core. Failed."

"And the game makers rebuilt it?"

"Brought it here along with the lesser Tyvarin and modified it," I said. "Probably installed behavioural overrides or some kind of neural dampening. But if the original mind is still in there..."

Clare went very still. "Then it's not just a monster."

Ba'quoo's voice pulsed through our minds again, laced with tension. *It descends. There is purpose in its flight. Not hunger. Not rage. Something colder.*

I looked up. The light through the crystal ceiling had changed – shadowed now, flickering with movement.

"I think it remembers what it was made for," I murmured. "But that doesn't mean it's beyond saving."

Clare turned to me, eyes wide. "Wait. That monster is coming to kill us. And you want to save it? How is that supposed to work?"

I didn't answer. Not yet. Because above us, something changed.

The light filtering through the crystalline veins in the ceiling dimmed, shadows sliding like liquid across the cavern floor. Then came the vibration – low, rhythmic, building from the stone itself like a second heartbeat.

Ba'quoo's feathers rippled and the chii around him scattered. *It comes. You must move. This place is not safe.*

The faintest tremor rippled through the crates stacked around us. Dust drifted from the high ledges. Somewhere above, something struck the mountain with enough force to make the entire cave shudder.

And then the diamonds in the ceiling – those slivers of light that had let in the morning sun – *fractured.*

Light speared inward as something enormous passed overhead. Not just wings. Not just mass. But presence.

Tyvaron had found us.

My mind went blank. I acted on instinct. I grabbed Clare around the waist, cradled her against my waist and sped towards the exit as fast as my coils allowed. I knew the chii would be fine. I had to protect my mate.

Drones would be waiting outside, but it was no longer safe in the cave. The ceiling could give in at any moment. If a second Tyvarin landed on the mountain... everything would crumble. I had to hurry.

"I can run!" Clare hissed, struggling against my hold on her.

"I know. But I am faster."

She muttered something beneath her breath but stopped complaining. She knew I was right. I may not have had legs, but I was bigger, stronger. I ignored the scrape of the diamond shards against my scales as I rushed us to the ledge leading to the tunnel we'd used last night. The gap in the rocks widened at our approach, giving way to freedom. And disaster.

We burst into the open.

The cold air slapped against my skin, sharp with the acrid tang of scorched rock. Clare squinted against the light, her arms instinctively wrapping tighter around me as I halted just short of the cliff's edge.

And there–spread across the sky like a dark tide–were the others.

Three. No, four.

Tyvarin.

Not as large as Tyvaron, but still massive. Wings like tattered banners. Serrated metal fused to organic bone. Their eyes glowed with the same cold fire–red pinpricks scanning the terrain below them. One circled low, releasing a hissing breath that ignited the treetops far down in the valley in a slow, crawling blaze.

Clare gasped. "Stars above..."

I coiled protectively around her, keeping us close to the entrance to the cave, sheltered below an outcrop. My mind raced. Tyvaron hadn't landed yet–but it didn't need to land to kill us. It could breathe fire.

"They're coordinating," I said grimly. "They're cutting off all escape routes. Even if we somehow make it down the mountain, we can't get through that fire."

Clare's hand touched my arm. "You said they had tactical minds. That they could think."

"They're not wild animals. They're weapons. And someone's giving the orders."

A high-pitched screech cut through the air. One of the lesser Tyvarin dove, unleashing a spiral of green fire. The blaze licked across the rocks and slammed into the cliff face below us. Stone cracked.

We had seconds.

I wrapped my arms tighter around Clare and turned, ready to bolt for cover.

Then the sky exploded.

A beam of focused light tore through the clouds. It struck the diving Tyvarin mid-wing, and the beast shrieked—mechanical and organic agony entwined. It spiralled, then slammed into the mountainside in a shower of stone and molten circuits.

The sound that followed sent a chill through my spine.

All doubt that these beasts were sentient vanished. It was in agony. And it was scared. I hoped it wouldn't suffer for long. It hadn't chosen to be here. None of us had. We were just pawns on the game makers' board.

Another sound, so loud it made me cower above Clare protectively.

A sonic boom. The sound of hope.

Clare looked up just as a sleek, angular shadow broke through the upper atmosphere—glowing engines blazing, its hull gleaming crimson and gold.

"Please tell me that's the Bloodstar," she whispered.

"It's one of their shuttles, I believe. I hope."

Another shot rang out—precise, clean. A second Tyvarin veered off, retreating into the clouds.

I didn't wait.

"This is our chance!" I shouted. "While they're regrouping!"

She nodded, already moving beside me.

We ran.

Behind us, the sky roared with fire and fury.

The shuttle swept down like a god of salvation, engines kicking up a cyclone of stone and ash. Clare coughed, shielding her face as I held her tight with one coil, steadying us against the blast.

The loading ramp extended mid-air, hissing open with a burst of steam. The shuttle didn't land – it hovered just low enough to make the jump possible.

A voice crackled through the external speaker, mechanical and unfamiliar. "Venom and Clare. Confirmed. Move before we get fried by a klatting firebeast!"

That did not sound like the game makers.

The Bloodstar's crew had come for us.

I tightened my hold on Clare. "Jump on my signal."

She didn't argue this time.

We leapt. My coils coiled and released, propelling us toward the open ramp. We landed hard, sliding on the metal surface as the platform began retracting the moment we were aboard.

Inside was dim, sterile. Straps and sealed crates lined the interior bay. The pilot remained unseen behind a shielded cockpit. No one rushed to greet us.

Clare sat down slowly, her breath shaky. "You... know these people?"

I shook my head while I engaged the automated seatbelt system to secure her safely into the seat. "Only through messages. I've never met them. They offered assistance – I didn't expect them to actually come."

She gave a soft, bitter laugh. "And me? I've been here the whole time. Woke up in a cryopod and the first being I met was a monster who wanted to use me as his toy. Still haven't spoken to a single human."

I reached for her hand. She let me hold it.

The shuttle pulled away from the mountain. I turned toward the narrow viewport in the rear bulkhead – just in time to see the sky darken.

Tyvaron.

He hovered above the cliff like a deity born of ruin – wings extended, body outlined in firelight. He didn't follow. Didn't roar. Just hovered, watching the shuttle as we pulled away.

And for a moment... he looked like a person. Not in form, but in intent. In restraint.

His glowing red eyes met mine.

I held my breath.

Then his wings folded, and he turned away – disappearing into the clouds with a trembling roar.

Clare whispered, "He let us go. He could have attacked the shuttle, but he didn't."

I nodded. "I think he did. He gave us a chance. Now we have to take it."

"We have to save the other women. Shut down the Trials. Punish those responsible."

My chest tightened at the passion in her voice. She could have turned from Kalumbu, run to a safe place, enjoyed her life. Instead, she was thinking of others. And of revenge.

I squeezed her hand. "I promise."

20

CLARE

Space was vast and black and mysterious. Throughout the entire flight, I'd expected someone to stop us, for a giant alien dragon to rip apart the shuttle, for space-ships to appear and block our way. But nothing happened. I craned my neck to look through one of the small porthole-like windows. The planet looked so beautiful from up here. The pastel colours and smooth lines of the continents told nothing of the pain, fear and death that happened on its surface.

"We're about to dock," the pilot announced. He hadn't said anything during the flight, but I'd been fine with that. I needed this moment of peace to come to terms with everything that had just happened.

I hope the chii are okay, I said in my head to test our mental connection. *I can't seem to reach them.*

Neither can I. We're too far now. But once we're on the Bloodstar I will contact them via their consoles and see if they require our help. I hope the game makers will simply forget about them now that we're gone. And hopefully, the game makers won't be in charge of the planet for much longer. Once they're gone, along with the monsters they brought to Kalumbu, the chii can live in the open again. Reclaim their planet for themselves.

I nodded and relaxed a little, enjoying the view of space from the porthole opposite. But it was no longer completely black. A strange grey sphere pushed into my field of view. No, there were several spheres, all bunched together like a giant caterpillar.

"Is that the Bloodstar?" I asked hesitantly. It looked nothing like I had imagined a spaceship to look. It wasn't all sleek lines and sharp angles like this shuttle. Instead, it was curvy and bumbly and strangely cute.

"Yes," came the pilot's voice. "That's my ship. Isn't she a beauty?"

With a metallic click, the ship shivered once, followed by a sharp hiss. The screen that had hid the cockpit slid open to our pilot.

He was huge. Hulking. Green. And he had tusks. Actual tusks.

I froze.

Was this another monster?

He caught my expression and gave me a friendly grin. "Don't worry, I'm the friendly kind of orc. Vruhag. I own this ship, and I'm not here to eat you."

Venom inclined his head. "Thank you for responding."

"You sent the right message. Silus is very impressed by your work. But you'll get to meet him in a click to talk all about coding stuff that I have no clue about." Vruhag tapped a glowing panel. "We're docked. Go on through. My crew will meet you."

"Crew?" I asked, still staring. I'd only ever seen other humans in cryopods or monsters trying to kill me. Not... this. I knew it was rude, but other than Venom and the chii, he was the first friendly alien I'd met.

Vruhag chuckled. "Don't worry, they're less green than me."

Venom took my hand. I followed him on unsteady feet through the opening hatch.

We stepped into a curving corridor that pulsed faintly with soft lights. It smelled of metal and clean air and something vaguely floral. I was still clutching the blanket Vruhag had tossed me during the flight.

At the end of the corridor, three people waited.

The first was a human woman – blonde hair cropped short, jacket military-tight, a blaster at her hip. She looked like she hadn't slept in a day, but her posture was iron-straight.

"Penny," she introduced herself. "You must be Clare and Venom."

The two others flanking her were more relaxed. Another human woman with warm brown skin and a nose ring – Pria, she said her name was – and a third I recognised only from the way Venom slightly relaxed at her presence.

"Fay," she said with a nod. "I know what it's like to come out of that hell."

They didn't ask questions. They didn't stare at me

like I was strange. They just handed me real clothes – a clean, soft jumpsuit – and offered water.

And when Penny turned to Venom, her voice softened. "Just so you know – an Intergalactic Authority warship is on its way. You're not alone anymore. We're not just rescuing people now. We're going to *end* this."

I blinked hard against the sting behind my eyes.

For the first time since I woke up in that metal coffin all alone, I had hope that this was going to turn out well in the end.

<hr>

They led us to the bridge for a proper meeting. Fay had offered to let us get some rest, freshen up and have some proper food, but both Venom and I were still buzzing with adrenaline and eager to know what was going to happen next. From Venom's reaction I'd gathered that having a warship here from the Intergalactic Authority, a sort of space police, was very unusual, yet also very wanted.

The bridge was bigger than I'd expected – a hemisphere cut in half by a smooth floor that seemed to suck up the noise of our footsteps, all sleek metal softened by warm lighting and huge windows interspersed with screens. Displays hummed softly across one wall, full of pulsing data streams, while five computer consoles were surrounded by other chairs and benches. This ship seemed to be built for a much larger crew than the presently assembled.

Venom paused beside me as we stepped in. His coils slowed. He looked... tense.

"Sit over here," Vruhag said, pointing at one of the benches. "Qong is just fixing us some snacks and will be here any minute. And this is Silus. I believe you've met."

A horned alien sitting at one of the consoles turned around, revealing the rest of his body. Holy moly. His lower half was furry and he had hooves. I tried not to stare, but it was difficult considering he was half-goat, half-man. His chest was bare and covered in brown hair, the same colour as his beard.

He grinned as soon as he saw Venom.

"You're the one who sent the root string with the fake KGM clearance code, aren't you?" he said. "That was brilliant."

Venom blinked. "You're Silus."

"Yup." He bounced once on his heels. "Been wanting to meet the ghost in Kalumbu's security for ages."

"Likewise," Venom said, relaxing a little next to me.

"Later," Vruhag cut in, stepping forward. "Let him breathe before you fry his brain."

He turned to Venom and held out a massive hand.

"You helped get me and Fay off that cursed planet. I don't forget debts like that."

Venom hesitated, then reached out and clasped the orc's forearm in a warrior's grip.

"I didn't do it for thanks," he said. "But I'm glad it worked."

"It worked because you let the Artep beam us up," Vruhag said. "And then you helped Silus get down onto the planet when he went against Twim's orders, and I'm almost sure you confused the ships that were pursuing us shortly after I picked up Silus and Pria from Kalumbu. I have never heard of a selfless naga before, but I am pleased to meet one."

"I had to," Venom replied. "And it wasn't selfless. I did it for Clare. There was no way I could save her myself. And the other females still on the space station."

Vruhag nodded solemnly, then turned to me. "You've been through more than most. You made it."

"I wouldn't have without him," I said quietly, glancing at Venom.

Silus hopped closer. "Okay, but seriously. Did you use the skewed-packet trick to override their network parity? Because I tried that once and–"

"Silus." Pria's voice was firm. "Later. Don't be such a geek."

He backed off with a sheepish grin.

Pria stepped forward. "I'm in charge of crew welfare. This ship is not a pleasure craft, but it's safe. You'll have privacy, food, a place to sleep. We don't have many rules, but one of them is this: survivors are family. If you're here, you've earned your place."

I swallowed the lump in my throat. "Thank you."

She nodded. "I wish we could tell you to retreat to a cabin and get some rest, but we have a bit of a situation going on here."

Silus snorted. "You can say that again. A second IA warship just showed up on my sensors. Vruhag, I think you should take the captain's chair and send them a message. We don't want them to think we're part of the game makers' fleet."

The bridge door hissed open again, and a new figure stepped through – tall, broad, and golden.

His skin gleamed like warm gold, its surface subtly patterned with a scale-like texture that reminded me uncannily of... waffles.

This had to be Qong, Penny's partner.

He carried a tray piled high with actual waffles, their buttery scent wafting across the room like an orgasm wrapped in sugar.

"Did someone mention snacks?" he asked, his deep voice a mellow rumble.

"That smells amazing," I said before I could stop myself, my stomach growling in enthusiastic agreement.

Pria grinned. "Apparently, this is what *he* smells like for Penny. Gofrens have a specific scent that mimics their mate's favourite food."

Penny blushed. "That's private." But she smiled at me before taking a plate from her golden partner.

Venom blinked but accepted a plate. I followed suit, still slightly stunned that a seven-foot golden waffle-man was handing me breakfast in space.

Qong handed out the rest of the plates and sat beside Penny, their arms brushing in quiet affection.

Silus licked syrup off his fingers with zero shame

and spun back to his console. "Still holding steady," he said, mouth full. "They haven't hailed again, but both IA ships are now approaching geosynchronous orbit over Kalumbu. Big ones. Proper warbirds. Venom, you know Kalumbu's fleet the best. Do they stand a chance against the IA ships?"

Venom exposed his fangs. "Maybe. Remember, they have hostages. Not just the Peritan females, but also hundreds of other contestants, some in cryosleep, others awake and ready to join the Trials. The IA has to follow strict laws. The game makers don't. If they threaten to kill the contestants...I'm not sure what the IA command will do. Honestly, I hope they find a different way to free them other than brute force. Lives will be lost either way. I can't see a peaceful solution."

Vruhag wiped his hands on a napkin and rose from the captain's chair, which creaked faintly beneath his bulk. He leaned toward the comm panel and pressed a button.

"This is the Bloodstar, independent vessel operating under humanitarian exemption protocols. We have recovered survivors from the Kalumbu Trials and are not affiliated with any sanctioned or unsanctioned operations on or around the planet. Please respond."

The pause was long enough for the air to feel heavy.

Then a crackle of static filled the room, followed by a clipped, authoritative voice.

"This is Commander Lhu of the Vigilance, acting representative of the Intergalactic Authority. We have received your transmission, Bloodstar. Stand by for boarding and interrogation. Maintain position and prepare for data transfer."

"Wait, let me," Venom said and rose from his chair. "Commander Lhu, this is Agent V-29@#1 of the IA Intelligence Fleet. I have been working under-cover on the Kalumbu Space Station until my discov-ery. If you check your records, you will find transmission from me including emergency broadcasts sent via my implant."

A pause followed his words. My heart was beating rapidly. What if they decided that we weren't friendly? They could blow us into smithereens.

"They're not taking chances," Penny muttered.

"They wouldn't," Vruhag said. "Kalumbu is a nightmare. They'll want to verify everything firsthand."

Silus rolled his shoulders. "I'm already compiling the files we extracted. Trial manifest, contestant tags, the genetic tracking records. Anything I could grab during my last hack. Maybe that will help."

Finally, Commander Lhu's voice filled the room again. "Agent V-29@#1, please activate your communi-cation implant for verification. We will send further instructions. If you do not respond within the next five clicks, we will assume that you are not who you say you are and will take appropriate measures."

With a click, the transmission ended. Silence followed.

Venom hissed in frustration. "I don't know if I can reactivate the implant that quickly. I need to focus.

Calm myself. It doesn't work if I'm agitated. Which I am. Very much."

The tension rolled off him in waves. He wouldn't be able to do it in this state. And we'd all die.

I took charge. "Everyone, get out. Venom needs space."

They all stared at me in surprise. Then, Vruhag got up from his captain's chair and gave me a court nod. "Do as she says. Clear the bridge."

21

VENOM

The world around me faded. I dropped inward – into the depths of thought, through the layers of consciousness and memory – until I stood once again before my mind safe.

I pressed my palm to the surface and thought the password. Once, twice, a third time for luck.

The safe opened.

Pain lanced through my skull as the dormant implant surged to life – a flare of pressure behind my eyes, my temples, the nape of my neck.

I didn't know how much time had passed. I was vaguely aware of Clare's presence, nestled against my side, her hand clutching mine. Without her, I would never have found the calm to enter the safe. She was my salvation. My everything. I hoped she would come to recognise that soon.

Dialling into the Vigilance's communications

network was surprisingly easy once I sent them my clearance codes.

I exhaled slowly.

"I'm in," I murmured aloud.

Clare squeezed my hand. "Was that it? You didn't even flinch."

I smiled without opening my eyes. "I had help."

A stocky male appeared in front of my mental eye, his face obscured in shadows. It was hard to guess his species. Exactly the point. Commander Lhu was so important that he did not reveal himself unless he absolutely had to. None of the IA commanders ever did.

"Agent Venom. I am pleased that you are indeed real and safely off that blasted station. What is the situation?"

"I have found sanctuary on the Bloodstar, along with several victims of the Trials' game makers. Did you receive the data I sent before I was caught by the enemy?"

"We have and it has been most useful. We also intercepted your message from the planet's surface, your witness statement. As unpleasant as your entry to the Trials must have been, it has provided us with hard evidence that contestants are indeed not taking part of their own free will. All in all, I believe we have enough data to put the game makers to trial."

A wave of pride washed over me. I had done it. All those rotations of isolation and deceit had been worth something.

"Commander Lhu, what are you planning to do now? Will you go for an outright attack?"

"Our strategists are still calculating the risk/benefit of various plans. We shall contact the Bloodstar if we need your assistance."

Sensing he was about to end the communication, I quickly interjected. "Are you aware there is at least one more Peritan female on the planet's surface? She was sent there just before Clare and me."

"We are aware. However, according to our calculation, there are at least 521 victims on the space station. They have to be our priority, along with capturing the remaining game makers. It is a pity Jarra can no longer be put to trial."

He vanished before I could respond. Pity my arse. I did not regret killing Jarra. He had threatened my mate. I only regretted that I had not killed him by burying my fangs deep in his throat.

I slowly opened my eyes only to look into the concerned face of my mate.

"Are you alright? You went very still and almost stopped breathing."

"I am fine. But... I could do with another waffle."

There was nothing to do but wait.

The others trickled back into the bridge shortly after our conversation with Commander Lhu ended.

Vruhag came first, nodding to me with a grunt of quiet respect. Then Silus, practically vibrating with half-swallowed energy. Pria, calm and practical. Penny and Qong entered together, hands brushing briefly. A tight circle of experience and scars. We were all survivors now.

But no one quite knew what came next.

Fay crossed her arms and broke the silence. "So? Do we sit on our hands while the IA makes their move, or do we start doing something useful?"

"They'll call when they need us," I said before anyone else could. "Until then, we don't jeopardise the mission by guessing."

"Agreed," Vruhag rumbled. "The last thing we want is to spook them into thinking we're some rogue operation."

Silus opened his mouth, likely to suggest exactly that, but Pria shot him a look. He reconsidered.

"Should we contact the chii now?" Clare asked. "I kind of miss them. And I want to make sure they're safe. I really hope the Tyvarin didn't attack their cave."

Fay's eyebrows shot up. "You met the chii?"

Clare nodded sadly. "Yes. We're mind-linked to two of them. And we never got to say a proper goodbye."

Fay smiled. "You don't have to. I speak to my chii, Ali'quii, all the time. The mental bond isn't strong enough to reach her from here while I'm awake, but as soon as I'm asleep, I can talk to her. At first, I thought it was just a dream, but then Vruhag experienced the same thing."

The orc nodded. "I asked them once whether they wanted us to take them along with us, once we'd rescued all the Peritan females. They saved our lives. We owe them a debt. But they have decided to stay on Kalumbu. It's their home."

I put an arm around Clare's shoulders. She leant into my touch as if she'd done it a thousand times before. My fangs ached with need. I wished we were alone, the two of us.

"I think it is best to wait until we go to sleep and try to contact them that way. The game makers will be on high alert just now, after our escape. If we were to send the chii a message, they might track our transmission. I don't want to endanger them."

Clare sighed. "That makes sense. I just hate waiting. I want to do something."

Fay turned to Clare and me. "Alright. While the rest of us avoid pacing holes into the floor, how about a proper tour? You've earned at least that."

We followed Fay through the corridors – all smooth curves and sloping tunnels. It reminded me of something organic, something grown rather than built. The Bloodstar had history in her bones.

She pointed out the canteen with its humming fabricator unit. I caught Clare's expression as the scent of waffles still lingered in the air, and my hearts did something strange. They fluttered. Briefly. Sharply.

We passed rooms lined with stars and screens,

virtual chambers and holo projections, a lounge that shimmered with rearranging furniture, even a swimming pool. Clare took it all in with wide eyes and cautious wonder. I had to remind myself that this was her first time on a spaceship. At least the first time that she was conscious. She had travelled so far to come here from her tiny planet, but she had been in cryosleep for that journey. I made a mental note to ask her later if she needed help with any of the ship's functions or if she had questions about how everything worked.

We stopped by the medbay for a few clicks so that Clare could get the tracker implant removed. She was a bit apprehensive going into one of the medpod – probably remembering waking up in the cryopod – but then squared her shoulders and followed the medical AI's instructions. The procedure was done almost instantly and caused her no pain. Still, it wasn't easy watching her lie in the pod, as if she was unwell.

Both of us were glad to leave the medbay and continue our tour. We passed a cosy observation lounge with huge windows showing Kalumbu and the stars beyond. I'd love to take Clare here one cycle and enjoy the view, preferably with a drink or two.

Then Fay stopped at a curved door.

"This is your cabin," she said with a smile. "Privacy settings are on. Use the panel if you need anything – food, light, temperature. There's even a playlist option, though fair warning, Qong's taste is... eclectic."

Clare smirked. "Trying to get rid of us?"

Fay winked. "Just giving you the space I wish I'd had when I got rescued."

She disappeared down the hall, leaving us in the sudden quiet.

The cabin lights adjusted as we entered – warm and dim, like sunset filtered through soft crystal. It reminded me of the chii's cave. The bed dominated the centre of the space, circular and low to the ground, its plush nest-like structure inviting. A round window offered a peaceful view of the stars. I was glad we couldn't see Kalumbu from here. I wanted to forget that blasted place.

Clare slowly turned to me. Her voice was playful but shaded with something deeper. "Still nothing to do but wait."

I let out a slow breath. This moment – unlike the chaos we'd escaped, the games we'd survived, the battles still ahead – was ours.

And I planned to savour it.

I moved forward, letting my coils unspool in a slow, smooth motion that kept me grounded while closing the distance between us. The floor was soft under my scales – some kind of alien foam or moss-textile. Warm. Comforting. My body welcomed it. But it wasn't the bed, or the lighting, or the silence that made my chest tighten.

It was her.

"You are safe now," I whispered. "*We* are safe now. We escaped. You could go anywhere. Explore the stars. Enjoy your freedom."

Her brow rose. "Are you trying to convince me to leave?"

"No." I swallowed. "Just reminding you that you have choices now."

"Could I go home? Would you take me?"

I stilled. A cold shiver ran over me.

She didn't know. I had to tell her. But it would ruin the moment.

Yet...it was selfish to keep the truth from her. She would find out soon. One of the other Peritans would make a comment in passing and she would discover the truth. It was better if I was the one to tell her.

"Clare...There is something you have to know."

She stepped closer. "What is it? Why do you sound so sad all of a sudden?"

"I don't know how to say this...Where to begin... You were abducted from your home planet a long time ago. Have you ever thought about that, space travel taking time, time passing differently, time-"

"Of course, I have," she interrupted me gently. "It was something Sa'quii said. *Lost in time.* I don't know much about space travel, but I have watched science fiction films. Unless they had a wormhole – do they exist?"

"They do." I couldn't help but smile.

"So, unless they had one of those, or some other means of travelling faster than light, it would take a long time to get here. I once read this article about the closest planet with possible life to Earth and that was something like four light years away. It would take a human spaceship tens of thousands of years to travel there. I doubt I was sleeping for that long, but..." She sighed deeply. "Just tell me. I know time has passed on Earth. I know my family, my friends, they probably all think I'm dead. Or are they...?"

I wrapped her into my arms and pulled her against my chest. "If my calculations are correct, you were abducted about seventy of your Peritan years ago."

She sucked in a sharp breath. "That is longer than I thought. But it also doesn't shock me. Not as much as I would have expected. I think I already said goodbye to the life I had when I lost my memories. Retrieving them was amazing, but they still feel sort of alien." She laughed softly. "Not that kind of alien, of course. But sometimes I remember something and I'm not sure if it's really me in that memory or someone else. Like they don't entirely match the person I am now."

I curled one of her midnight locks around my fingers. "You are so strong. I am so very proud of you."

Clare snuggled against my chest. "I could go all hysteric and start to cry, but what's the point? I'm glad to have my memories back. I can look at them and remember my old life. But now, I want to forge a new life." She traced the scales on my chest with her delicate fingers. My fangs hurt with need and my cocks were pushing against their protective sheath.

Wrong moment to get aroused. She needed me to process what she'd just been told. This was not the time to claim her as my mate, as much as I craved that.

"And what if I choose to stay?" Her voice was quiet but steady. "With you?"

I had no answer for that – not one that wouldn't come out raw.

Instead, I reached for her hand. Gently. Slowly. As if she might still change her mind.

She didn't pull away.

The moment her fingers curled into mine, something inside me loosened. I hadn't realised how tightly I'd been holding myself together – how every breath since that cave had been measured, calculated, restrained. For her safety. For mine.

I pressed her hand to my chest – not just to the place where one heart beat, but the other, too. Both. Fast. Alive.

"You calm them," I said. "Both of them. It's never happened before."

Her eyes softened. "I think you calm mine, too."

A silence bloomed between us.

"I've never shared a space like this," I admitted. "Never invited someone into a nest. Into a... home. At some point, we might leave the Bloodstar and go elsewhere, but I have a feeling we might stay here for a while."

"I kind of like it here," she said. "Our own cosy cabin just for us and then a whole big spaceship with waffle machines and swimming pools and people who are on our side."

Her fingers squeezed mine. My hood flared slightly, the instinctive signal of openness. Trust.

I didn't kiss her. Not yet. Instead, I ran the back of my hand along her jaw – a slow, reverent stroke that said *I'm here. You're safe. We're real.*

Her breath caught.

And then, just like before, she reached up, put a hand around my neck and pulled me down until our lips met.

22

CLARE

The kiss started slow. Not tentative – we'd already crossed that line – but reverent, like he was tasting something he thought he might never be allowed to have again.

Venom's lips were warm against mine, his fangs just barely brushing my bottom lip, careful and restrained. I cupped his cheek with one hand, the other pressed to the firm plane of his chest. He didn't push. He didn't rush. He let me decide.

And I did.

I parted my lips and leaned in deeper.

The low sound he made – something between a growl and a sigh – rumbled through my bones. His arms came around me, strong and sure, his coils tightening just enough to cradle, not trap.

"I've never claimed anyone," he murmured against my mouth. "But I want to claim you. With teeth. With heat. With everything I am."

My breath hitched. "Then stop waiting."

But he didn't move. Not yet.

His gaze burned into mine – not with heat, but with something deeper. Ancient. Sacred.

"There's something you need to know first," he said, voice low and reverent. "If I take you now, fully... if I bite you... it won't just be physical. It's not just sex for my kind."

I blinked. "You said before that it is some kind of bond."

He nodded once. "More than a bond. It ties us. Soul to soul. You'd become mine. My mate. My clan would recognise you as one of us. It's not reversible. Not breakable. You'd be part of me, and I part of you. Even across galaxies."

My heart thudded. "Is that what you want?"

His voice was barely a whisper. "Yes. More than I've ever wanted anything."

I swallowed hard. "And what else does it mean? Besides soul-bonding?"

"It means protection," he said. "It means family. You'd be accepted by any naga as one of our own. It also means... potential. A future. If we ever wanted children, the bond would allow that. Without it, the chances are...non-existent."

Children.

I hadn't thought that far ahead. How could I? But the idea didn't scare me as much as it should have. Not with him. Not now.

"So, if I say yes," I said slowly, "you bite me, and I become yours. Forever."

"Yes," he said. "And I become *yours*. But only if you want it. Only if you choose."

His tail curled gently around my wrist, not pulling, just anchoring me to this moment.

"Do you?" he asked. "Choose me?"

I looked into his eyes – slitted, glowing faintly, full of fierce devotion and something that felt a lot like love.

And I knew.

"Yes," I said. "I choose you."

His breath shuddered out of him like I'd just released something he'd been holding for too long.

Venom moved slowly, reverently, lowering me into the softness of the bed. The sheet was warm and silky, gently supporting my body. His coils cradled my legs and hips, lifting me into his touch. His hands traced down my body, slowly undressing me like I was something sacred – not hurried, not hungry, just... careful. Worshipful.

When I was naked, I looked up at him. His eyes were dark with lust and desire. Yet he was holding back. He was going slow for my sake. And I loved him for it.

Yes.

That word.

So small, so deep, so intense.

His hands ran up and down my arms. I trembled beneath his touch, not from fear but anticipation. My skin felt too tight for the heat gathering beneath it.

He pressed a kiss to my sternum, another just beneath my ribs. Lower still.

"I want to know you," he whispered, the forked tip of his tongue flicking softly against the inside of my thigh. "Every breath. Every sound. Every taste."

My breath caught.

He shifted between my legs, his coils bracing my thighs apart with a gentleness that still held strength. And then – fuck me – his tongue. That split, forked tongue sliding through me like tense silk. He didn't rush. He teased, explored, circled.

I gasped. My hips bucked against his mouth.

"Please," I whispered. "Venom..."

He growled softly. His tail tightened a little around my waist, one loop pressing me closer, another sliding up to curl over my breast, teasing my sensitive folds in rhythm with his tongue.

Every movement was calculated, patient. Like he was memorising what made me gasp, what made my body tremble, what made my fingers tighten into the sheet.

When he finally pulled back, I was shaking – aroused beyond thought, strung tight with need. My entire body was a live wire, sparking wherever he touched.

He rose above me, eyes burning. His voice was thick with restraint.

"You're ready for me. But if I go further... I will mark you. Mate you. No going back."

I reached up, cupped his face. "I said yes."

His hood flared. His fangs gleamed.

And then he lowered himself again – this time, not with tongue.

But with all of him.

I felt the first press of him – thick, hot, unyielding – and gasped. This wasn't the same as before. This cock was even thicker, stretching me to the limit, and the ridges around it felt more like bumps that would give me the ultimate pleasure when he fully entered me. And this was deeper, slower, more deliberate. He was holding back again, despite everything.

"You're shaking," he murmured, brushing a kiss across my collarbone. "You can still say no."

"I'm shaking because I want you," I whispered. "Because I'm ready."

A rumble built in his chest. His forked tongue flicked out, brushing my bottom lip as his tail resumed its gentle tease across my breast and down my hip. Its tip settled against my clit, stroking gently but firmly. Preparing me again, even though I already ached for him.

Then I felt it – the moment he let go of whatever part of himself he'd been holding back.

He sank into me, inch by beautiful inch, and my breath caught as my body adjusted around him. His cock felt like nothing I'd ever known. Yet it was everything I needed. Everything I wanted.

I felt utterly filled. Claimed.

And yet, I knew this was only part of what he could give.

His voice was tight with strain. "I'm only using one. If I used both... not yet."

My mouth parted. "Later?"

He chuckled, low and raw. "Later, my little mate. When you can take it. When you want it."

He began to move. Slow, deep thrusts that sent ripples of pleasure through me, building something vast and inevitable. His tail coiled beneath my spine, lifting my hips just enough to change the angle, to make me feel every ridge, every twitch.

But it wasn't just his body. It was his eyes, locked on mine. His hands, reverent on my skin. His hearts, beating in sync with my own.

I was on the edge, trembling, when he leaned close to my throat.

"I'm going to bite you now," he murmured. "I'll be gentle. But it will bind us. Soul to soul. Forever."

I nodded, not trusting my voice.

His lips brushed against the nape of my neck, kissing my burning skin. Then his fangs sank in – just a pinch, sharp but fleeting – and something ancient surged through me. Not pain. Not even heat. More like light. A connection forged not through words or gestures but something deeper. Soul-deep.

My orgasm slammed into me, tearing through my body like lightning. I cried out, and he held me, moved with me, followed me over the edge.

He shuddered with release, his grip tightening, his body locking to mine as his second heart thundered against my ribs. I felt the pulse of him inside me, deep and anchoring. A claiming. A promise.

We were mates. We were everything.

We stayed like that, tangled together in a nest of limbs and coils and breath, until the stars outside the window were just a blur.

I drifted between warmth and dreams, wrapped in Venom's arms, his coils a steady pressure around me. I could feel the bond between us – not just on my skin where his fangs had marked me, but *in* me. A thread of silver warmth connecting my heartbeat to his.

Sleep pulled me under gently.

And in the dream, I was not alone.

The air shimmered in warm, comforting sunshine. I stood beneath purple trees. It was so real that I could smell the moss, the flowers, even the tree bark.

Venom appeared beside me, his hand already in mine. His eyes glowed, not with danger or desire now, but with something tender. I could feel our connection simmering faintly between us.

Then I felt her.

Sa'quii.

She walked along the jungle floor with her elegant gait, tails erect and moving in hypnotising patterns. Her three eyes blinked slowly in welcome.

You are safe. Her voice was as warm as always.

"We are," I said aloud in the dream. "We made it off the planet."

Venom nodded. "We're aboard a ship. The Bloodstar. The Intergalactic Authority is here. They're preparing to strike against the game makers."

Her feathers rippled with interest. *They have not come here yet.*

"No," I said, stepping forward. "And we will try and make sure they don't."

I didn't know why I suddenly felt the urge to protect the chii from the IA, but I'd learned to trust my instincts.

Venom nodded in agreement. "We will not reveal your existence to the IA. We promise. Kalumbu should belong to its own people. Not become another outpost or colony."

She chirped softly. *Thank you.*

"Are the others okay? Ba'quoo?" I asked. "Tyvaron didn't hurt anyone?"

The trees behind her shimmered with new colours – hundreds of golden, bronze and silver chii, their outlines somewhat fuzzy, but the message was clear. They were safe.

They left. The sky-beasts were summoned, but their hearts were not aligned with the hunters. Part of the forest is burned, but none of us were harmed.

Relief poured through me.

Venom tightened his fingers around mine. "Then I hope that soon, you will be able to live freely again. Out in the open. No more need to hide."

Sa'quii padded forward. Her feathered tails brushed against my hand.

You both carry light now. Stronger together. You have bonded.

I blushed. "We have."

You will change this world. Maybe more.

I felt it then – a faint ripple of energy as the dream began to pull apart at the edges. The way it always did when dawn approached.

"We'll come back one day," I promised. "Not to interfere. Just to see you again."

We will be here.

Her voice lingered even as the dream melted into mist.

23

VENOM

TWO CYCLES LATER

The station smelled sterile. Not clean, not new. Sterile. Scrubbed of identity. Every surface was white, metallic, neutral. No sign of the cruelty it had once harboured. No blood. No bodies. Just silence.

A false kind of peace.

I stood at Clare's side, our fingers lightly touching. She hadn't let go of me since we'd stepped off the Bloodstar's shuttle. Her heart beat steadily through our bond – a soft thrum of nerves, grief, and something stronger.

Resolve.

She didn't flinch at the sight of the cryopods. She didn't falter when the first woman was woken. She just spoke to her in the gentlest voice I'd ever heard, told her where she was, what had happened, and that she was safe now.

Safe.

The IA had worked fast. With the help of two more battle cruisers, they'd dismantled the command structure, locked down the game makers and their lackeys, freed the contestants from their cells, and started cataloguing the monsters and contestants still on the planet's surface. Most of the perpetrators were in custody. A few had tried to flee or fight. They hadn't succeeded.

Justice, at last. Or the beginning of it.

Clare moved to the next pod while Pria and Penny supported a trembling woman behind her. Fay and Qong were comforting a small group by the wall, helping them sip water, making quiet conversation. Silus had disappeared into the tech wing with a gleam in his eyes – likely trying to hijack the station's entertainment system to broadcast his favourite satyr music.

I exhaled.

The Bloodstar crew didn't just survive. They *healed*. And now, they were helping others do the same.

"You look like a commander," a low voice said behind me.

I turned. Vruhag stood with his arms crossed, his stance easy but his gaze watchful.

"I've never commanded anyone," I replied. "Only codes."

"Same thing, sometimes," he said. "But you helped win a revolution, Venom. Maybe not with weapons. But with truth."

I dipped my head in acknowledgement. "It's not over yet. Not everyone is safe yet. And the game makers need to face justice. They need to pay for what they did."

"Yes," he agreed. "But we've taken their power. And we're not giving it back."

He handed me a datapad. "Commander Lhu wants us to stay."

I raised an eyebrow. "Stay?"

"Take over management of the station. Convert it into a sanctuary. Somewhere survivors can stay until they're ready to decide what's next. Somewhere we can monitor the region. They're offering back pay, resources, autonomy. The game makers' assets have been liquidated. The IA is giving us some of those credits to turn this place from one of fear into one of hope."

"And the Bloodstar crew?"

"They already voted. Unanimously. They want to stay. Help. Build something better. Now only you and your mate have to decide."

I looked at Clare across the room, gently holding a newly awakened woman's hand. Empathy and confidence streamed from her, as bright as a star. She lit up this place. And my hearts.

"I will talk to Clare. It is up to her, but I am willing to stay. At some point, I want to show her my planet, my home, but for now, there is much to do here. I know this station better than any of you. I want to help."

Vruhag clapped my shoulder, hard enough to nearly stagger me. "Good. Talk to her. And Venom... Get some rest. You deserve it."

It took me a while to persuade Clare that she deserved a break. Only the promise of showing her my old cabin got her to leave the Peritan females and accompany me away from this part of the station.

We took a lift down three levels. It smelled just as sterile as everything else.

The corridors were quieter here. Most of the rescued women were being kept in the medical wing or the recovery lounge. This wing – the old staff quarters – still smelled of menace and secrets.

"I used to live here," I said as we passed the locked doors. "During the early rotations of my infiltration."

Clare followed close, her hand brushing mine. "This is where you worked?"

I nodded. "And where I pretended to be someone I wasn't. I played my role so well that I got promoted pretty quickly."

We stopped in front of a black panelled door. I entered the code, surprised that it still worked. They had blocked my access codes for most of the systems, but nobody had expected me to return to my old room.

The lights flickered on.

My quarters were exactly as I'd left them: minimalist, cold, sleek. The bed was a firm cot against one wall, the desk a sprawl of cables and encrypted terminals. Data chips were scattered like shrapnel. The walls were bare, save for a single screen showing security feeds from the station's lower decks – a relic of paranoia

I'd never disabled. A few weights lay discarded on the floor. There were no personal effects. No pictures of my family, nothing soft or gentle.

Clare stepped inside and let out a low breath. "It's... efficient."

"It's empty," I said. "Because I was empty. I built this persona – the cold hacker naga who didn't care who got hurt, as long as the credits came in. That's what they needed. That's who they feared. And so, that's who I became."

She walked over to the desk, picked up a small chip between her fingers. "Did it work?"

"Yes," I said quietly. "But I lost pieces of myself in the process. Or I thought I did. Until I met you."

She looked at me and her expression softened. "You never were this person with me. You can let go of him now. Those days are over."

"I don't want this place to be what it was," I told her. "I want to transform it. With you. Turn these corridors into homes. These surveillance rooms into gardens. Make it a place of healing. The IA have offered us to take control of the station. Turn it into a sanctuary for everyone hurt by the Trials."

Her voice was soft. "You think we can?"

"I think," I said, stepping toward her, "that we have already started. One room at a time."

Clare looked around again – the sterile corners, the blinking consoles, the dusty silence.

Then she smiled.

"Let's do it. Let's make this place ours."

Her smile was infectious. With her, I could do this. I didn't want to live in this cabin ever again, but I could imagine making a home somewhere else on the station. Somewhere with a bigger bed.

Clare wandered to the far side of the room and brushed her fingers over one of the dark panels. "Did you ever think you'd come back here? That you'd survive?"

"No," I admitted. "There were many cycles when I didn't expect to make it to the next. But I always had something to hold on to."

She turned to me, curiosity flickering in her eyes. "Your mission?"

"Not just that." I hesitated. Then crossed to the desk and reached for a small, recessed panel near the base of the terminal.

A flick of my tail tip revealed a hidden port. My tail was the key to it. Nobody else could access it. The screen hummed to life with a soft blue glow.

Clare stepped beside me as lines of code scrolled across the screen, then dissolved, revealing an image I hadn't looked at in far too long.

It was a photograph: grainy, natural light, taken in the lush valleys of Serpenthyra.

My family.

My father coiled proudly at the centre, scales a deep obsidian blue. My mother beside him, her hood flared in laughter, silver-green patterns swirling across her skin. Behind them, my twin brothers – taller than me, broader, competitive as hell – and my sister, youngest of us all, her tail looped protectively around a nest of glowing moss.

Clare leaned in. "They're beautiful."

"They're my clan," I said softly. "My family. And now... you are too."

She looked at me, her expression unreadable for a beat. Then she smiled – small, fierce, and utterly sincere.

"Thank you for showing me," she said. "I want to know everything about them. About you. About the naga you were before this mission."

I rested my forehead lightly against hers, breathing her in.

"I will tell you everything," I whispered. "And one day, once we have erased all the sadness of Kalumbu and replaced it with something better, I will take you to Serpenthyra to meet them."

Our communicator bands flashed and vibrated at the same time.

>>*Meet in the command centre. V.*<<

"He needs to start writing his full name," Clare laughed. "Vruhag and Venom, it's going to get confusing."

I grinned at her. "I was here first. And I am the only V for you."

We headed towards the command centre which was right next to the room I had worked in before I'd been discovered. Full circle.

The command centre hadn't changed since I'd last stood here while reporting to my superiors – not in structure, at least. But the atmosphere was different. The cold weight of secrets and repression had been replaced by something warmer.

Purpose. Hope. Love.

The entire crew was assembled. Vruhag at the helm, arms crossed, eyes scanning the screens with a kind of calm he hadn't worn on Kalumbu. Fay stood at his side, fingers interlaced with his. Silus lounged at a console, for once not hacking anything – having Pria on his lap would have made that difficult. Penny and Qong sat close together, their shoulders brushing, golden textured skin and dark hair glowing beneath the artificial lights.

Clare and I stepped in, hand in hand.

Vruhag gave us a nod. "Good timing. The IA just sent final confirmation."

He tapped the central console, and a crisp, authoritative voice filtered through the speakers – Commander Lhu.

"By decision of the Intergalactic Authority Oversight Council, stewardship of Kalumbu and its orbiting facility is hereby granted to the independent vessel Bloodstar and her crew. The facility will be registered as a protected sanctuary. Resources, guards, and quarterly credits will be dispatched effective immediately. All claims to the planet are suspended under IA law until further reassessment.

"You have done what many thought impossible. You have made Kalumbu more than a battleground. You've made it a future. Let us hope that there will be no second Kalumbu. We have shown the criminal underworld that their time is numbered. And while the IA will pursue justice in the courts and undercover, the Bloodstar crew has the authority to help the victims here on the former Kalumbu Station. One of our strategists has suggested a new name for it. Beacon. A light in the darkness to guide those who need it to their new home."

The message ended with a soft chime.

We all stood in silence.

Then Penny exhaled. "Well... I guess this is home now."

Clare stepped closer to the viewport, her gaze fixed on the pastel marble of Kalumbu far below. "There's still so much pain down there. So many ghosts. But maybe... this is how it starts. With people who care."

"We do care," I said, curling my tail lightly around her legs. "And we're not alone anymore."

Qong spoke up, his voice slow and deliberate. "Maybe Kalumbu isn't just where we were broken. Maybe it's where we begin again."

Vruhag grunted. "Then let's begin. Together."

The screen dimmed as the station adjusted orbit, the view of Kalumbu slowly tilting beneath us — glowing with clouds, alive with the promise of change.

Clare leaned against me, warm and solid and full of light. I wrapped her in my arms and rested my chin on her head, before whispering so softly that only she could hear.

"I love you. Now and forever. I never thought I'd

have a mate. Didn't think I deserved one. But then I found you. You were my beacon. The star that guided me back into the light."

She turned to look up at me, her eyes shining with the same love I felt in my hearts.

"You didn't need me to guide you. You were already in the light. You are a good person, Venom. You just forgot that for a while."

Together, we looked down on Kalumbu. The planet that had brought us together. It had given us fear and pain but also hope and joy. A planet wasn't evil. It was the people who ruled over it.

"Home," Clare whispered. "This is our home."

"Yes. And even when we leave here, I will always be home. My home is with you, Clare. You are my mate, now and always."

"You're so cheesy," she laughed, but then she wrapped her hands around my hood and pulled me close. Our lips hovered a breath apart when she whispered what I'd craved her to say.

"But you're also mine. My mate. Venom."

Pain.

Heat.

Smoke in my throat.

Metal claws at my mind.

I disobeyed. They scream inside my head. It hurts. They don't stop.

I should have killed. I should have burned them.

I did not.

The small ones live. The ones they fear. The ones they hate.

I was told to kill and I did not.

Because I remembered.

A flicker. A scent.

Soft skin. Warm breath.

Small hands. A voice like light.

Not prey. Not enemy.

Different.

Mine.

The fire inside me stirs. Old. Faint.

From before the metal. Before the pain.

I crawl back to my cave. To stone. To dark. To quiet.

My wing drags. My bones crack. My fire is weak.

Pain is everything.

But she is close.

I feel her.

I hear her breath beneath the stone.

The pain will return.

The chains will pull.

But for now... I breathe.

And I remember.

And I hope.

***

My beta readers were very insistent on getting another spicy scene, this time with both you-know-what...
Download the bonus scene here:
skyemackinnon.com/naga-bonus

This is the end of Clare and Venom's story, but it is not the end of the Starlight Monsters series!
Continue with My Big Grumpy Alien Dragon!

This is only one of many series set in the Starlight Universe. How about some alien Highlanders (Starlight

Highlanders), *Vikings* (Starlight Vikings), *Pirates* (Alien Abduction for Pirates) *or alien reverse harem* (The Intergalactic Guide to Humans, Vol. 1)?

For all the latest releases, author updates and cat pictures, subscribe to my newsletter:
skyemackinnon.com/newsletter

This book is part of the Starlight Universe, an entire galaxy filled with hunky aliens, exotic planets, and the human women ready to find love among the stars.

Starlight Highlanders Mail Order Brides

Alien Highlanders in kilts come to Earth in search of brides... and take them to planet Albya. Three m/f standalones full of humour, action and steamy romance. Part of the Intergalactic Dating Agency.

Starlight Vikings

Set on Earth and on the spaceship Valkyr, this trilogy of m/f standalones is all about hunky alien Vikings in need of females. Part of the Intergalactic Dating Agency.

Starlight Mermen

Hundreds of years ago, they crash-landed on Earth

and gave rise to many of our legends. Now, they're back, desperate for female mates. Part of the Intergalactic Dating Agency.

The Intergalactic Guide to Humans

A humorous take on alien abductions, probing and other shenanigans. One reverse harem trilogy about clueless aliens and the human woman they abducted, followed by several standalone romances with various pairings (m/f, f/m/f and m/m). If you want light entertainment filled with unicorns, fabulous misunderstandings and unusual body parts, this is the series for you.

Starlight Monsters

These aliens are not your usual humanoids... they have claws, fangs, tails, scales, knotty dicks and will growl at you. Interconnected m/f standalones with lots of action, steam and fated mates.

ABOUT THE AUTHOR

Skye MacKinnon is a Scottish romance author who was raised by elves in the mystical Highlands and calls the Loch Ness monster her friend. Her bestselling books weave together romance with action, suspense and whimsical humour, creating page-turners filled with strong heroines, alpha heroes and loveable monsters.

Whether she's writing about aliens in kilts, hunky Vikings or cat shifter assassins, Skye likes to put a new spin on familiar tropes. Some of her heroines don't have to choose, some fall in love with other women, and others get abducted by clueless aliens.

Skye lives with her bossy cat on the west coast of Scotland and uses the dramatic views from her office as an inspiration, no matter whether she writes fantasy, paranormal or science fiction romance. Until she gets abducted by aliens, that is.

Subscribe to her newsletter:
skyemackinnon.com/newsletter

Find all of Skye's books on her website,
skyemackinnon.com, where you can also order signed
paperbacks and swag.

Many of her books are available as audiobooks.

SCIENCE FICTION ROMANCE

Set in the Starlight Universe

- **Starlight Vikings** (sci-fi m/f romance)
- **Starlight Mermen** (sci-fi m/f romance)
- **Starlight Monsters** (sci-fi m/f romance)
- **Starlight Highlanders Mail Order Brides** (sci-fi m/f romance)
- **The Intergalactic Guide to Humans** (sci-fi romance with various pairings)

Set in other worlds

- **Between Rebels** (sci-fi reverse harem set in the Planet Athion shared world)
- **The Mars Diaries** (sci-fi reverse harem)
- **Aliens and Animals** (f/f sci-fi romance co-written with Arizona Tape)

PARANORMAL & FANTASY ROMANCE

- **Claiming Her Bears** (post-apocalyptic shifter reverse harem)
- **Daughter of Winter** (fantasy reverse harem)
- **Catnip Assassins** (urban fantasy reverse harem)
- **Infernal Descent** (paranormal reverse harem based on Dante's Inferno, co-written with Bea Paige)
- **Seven Wardens** (fantasy reverse harem co-written with Laura Greenwood)
- **The Lost Siren** (post-apocalyptic, paranormal reverse harem co-written with Liza Street)

OTHER SERIES

- **Academy of Time** (time travel academy standalones, reverse harem and m/f)
- **Defiance** (contemporary reverse harem with a hint of thriller/suspense)

STANDALONES

- Song of Souls – m/f fantasy romance, fairy tale retelling
- Highland Butterflies – sapphic romance
- Wings of Time and Fate - epic fantasy

BOX SETS

- Daggers & Destiny – a fantasy romance starter library
- Stars & Seduction - a science fiction romance starter library

9 781917 585170